DEATH NEVER STRIKES TWICE

Suspecting his wife Janine of having an affair, businessman Charles Jensen hires private eye Johnny Merak to follow her. Merak learns that Jensen had divorced his first wife Arlene — who has since disappeared . . . Convinced that Jensen had arranged Arlene's murder, Arlene's sister, Barbara Winton, also approaches Merak to investigate. Ignoring warnings to drop his investigations, he's knocked unconscious, and wakes next to a woman's corpse — a woman who has been shot with his gun. Then the police arrive . . .

Books by *John Glasby*
in the *Linford Mystery Library*:

THE SAVAGE CITY
A TIME FOR MURDER

JOHN GLASBY

◆

DEATH NEVER STRIKES TWICE

A Johnny Merak mystery thriller *JMC*

Complete and Unabridged

LINFORD
Leicester

First published in Great Britain

First Linford Edition
published 2007

British Library CIP Data

Glasby, John S. (John Stephen)
Death never strikes twice.—Large print ed.—
Linford mystery library
1. Private investigators—Fiction
2. Murder—Investigation—Fiction
3. Detective and mystery stories
4. Large type books
I. Title
823.9'14 [F]

ISBN 978–1–84617–835–1

Published by
F. A. Thorpe (Publishing)
Anstey, Leicestershire

Set by Words & Graphics Ltd.
Anstey, Leicestershire
Printed and bound in Great Britain by
T. J. International Ltd., Padstow, Cornwall

This book is printed on acid-free paper

1

It was one of those hot, still days in late July when the heat lay like a smothering shroud over the city. I'd had the windows open all day but it made little difference. Even now, with the sun going down, the temperature was still in the eighties.

Business had been slack for over a fortnight. Either the bad guys were staying indoors with the air conditioning working overtime, minding their own business, or they had migrated further along the coast. I lit a cigarette and checked my watch. A little after six-thirty.

There had been a solitary fly buzzing around the light bulb ever since I'd come in that morning. Now it had decided the heat was too much for such strenuous exercise and it was crawling slowly around the top of my desk.

My secretary, Dawn Grahame, had left half an hour earlier and I was on the point of closing up for the day, just locking my filing cabinet, when there came a knock on the door. It was a polite kind of knock, unlike the usual kind whenever anyone came calling for the rent.

I recognized the guy who walked in at once. His picture had been in the papers often enough. Charles Henry Jensen III, one of the really big names in L.A. society. He was about forty, I reckoned. Well dressed, but nothing flash. His dark hair was greying a little around the temples but that only served to give him a distinguished look. There was a big gold ring on his finger and a diamond stud in his tie.

Even him being there gave me a funny feeling. He wasn't the sort of client I normally had walk into the office.

He stood just inside the doorway, saying nothing, as if wondering whether he'd come to the right place. His eyes were never still, taking in everything.

'Mister Merak?' he said finally.

I nodded. 'That's what the name on the door says.' I motioned him to the chair in front of the desk. While he pulled it out and sat down, I raked through my memory files for everything I knew about him. It wasn't much. There certainly wasn't anything to explain why he was there.

Head of the Jensen Construction Corporation, founded more than seventy years before by his grandfather. From what I'd read, he was one of the richest men in the city with a personal fortune of several hundred million dollars. Twice married and the divorce from his first wife had been acrimonious to say the least. Now apparently happily married to his second. None of that gave me the slightest hint of why he'd come to see me.

Delicately brushing an invisible piece of fluff from his expensive suit, he said, 'You're probably wondering why I'm here, Mister Merak.'

'The thought had crossed my mind,' I replied, easing myself into my chair. 'It isn't often I have someone like you wanting my services.'

'No, I guess not. I've made some inquiries about you. I hope you don't mind but I like to know who I'm dealing with.'

'Sure. But if it's a private eye you want, with your dough and connections, I'd have expected you to hire one of those slick investigators rather than a one-man show like me.'

He gave me a faint smile. 'I've already had one of them. He wasn't worth the money I paid him.'

'Then what makes you think I'll be any better?' I reached for the matches and relit my cigarette.

'I need someone who's good at his job and can keep his mouth shut. From what I've been told, I figure you fit into that category.'

I opened the bottom drawer of my desk and took out the half-empty bottle of Scotch and a couple of glasses. I held out the bottle towards him. When he shook his head, I poured a drink for myself. A little early in the evening, I told myself, but what the hell — ?

Jensen sat forward a little in his chair. He looked strangely uneasy. He had something important on his mind and he wasn't quite sure how to spill it.

'You probably know I've been married twice,' he began. He sounded as though he was making a confession to a priest. 'And my first marriage hit the rocks not long after the wedding. Arlene was a gold-digger of the first degree. She wanted money and what it could buy. Nothing else.'

'It happens like that now and again,' I assured him.

He gave me a funny look. Then he went on, 'I thought it would be different with Janine. At first, I guess it was. Then I found out she's no better than Arlene. Sisters under the skin. The rows started, sometimes going on all night. Pretty soon, I wasn't able to concentrate properly on the business. And it's getting progressively worse.

'Oh, as far as our friends are concerned, we're the ideal couple. She's an excellent hostess, never puts a foot wrong. But it didn't take me long to figure there's someone else in the picture. She's taken to going away at weekends, ostensibly to visit her sister in Cleveland.'

5

'And you know that's not the case?'

'I know damned well she's seeing someone else. But she's clever, damnably clever. So far I've not got a single shred of evidence to her adultery. That private detective I hired found absolutely nothing.'

I took a swallow of the whisky. 'Maybe there's nothing to find,' I suggested.

His eyes flashed dangerously at that remark. I guessed I'd hit a raw nerve somewhere. 'Believe me, there's plenty if I can only find someone capable of looking for it. Someone like you, Merak. You're not scared of side-stepping the law if it suits you.'

I ran his proposition through my mind. It wasn't too different from several cases I'd worked on in the past. But, somehow, I got the feeling there was a lot he wasn't telling me. Digging up the dirt on straying wives and husbands was certainly in my line of business. But I liked to know everything at the very beginning. Otherwise I felt like a blind guy without a white stick, blundering aimlessly along dead ends.

'Okay, I'll take the job,' I told him. 'But it may take a little time. I'll want to know beforehand when she's about to visit this so-called sister of hers. And I'll need a recent photograph of her.'

'Of course.' He fumbled inside his breast pocket and brought out his wallet. Extracting a photograph, he handed it to me.

She was a stunning blonde. Aged around twenty-eight, I guessed. She was smiling, showing a set of perfect teeth. I had the impression she smiled a lot, but her eyes held a deep look. She was a woman who thought deeply and carefully about everything she did. Nothing impetuous about her actions. The mouth was wide with a full lower lip. Yet there was a hint of hardness to it that made me think. She was also used to having what she wanted and didn't care overmuch about how she got it.

'At least she shouldn't be too difficult to pick out in a crowd,' I remarked.

Jensen replaced his wallet. 'I want everything you can get on her. Who she sees, where she goes, what she does. I don't just want dates and places. I want names in hotel registers, taped recordings, infrared pictures. Concrete proof that'll stand up in court.'

'Another divorce?' I asked.

'Naturally.' He almost snarled the word. 'And there'll be no alimony this time. I can hire half a dozen slick city lawyers to claim adultery so she won't be entitled to a single cent. But it's up to you to get me the proof I need.'

He smiled again and this time there was something at the back of it I didn't like. I couldn't figure out exactly what it was. Revenge? Maybe, or perhaps something more sinister.

I finished my drink and set the empty glass down on the desk. 'My usual fee for this kind of case is — '

He lifted a hand. 'I don't quibble about money when it's in a good cause, Mister Merak. I'll give you a five thousand dollar retainer and whatever your usual fees and expenses are, I'll double them. Just get me what I need — and as quickly as possible.'

I got up. 'I'll make a start on it right

away,' I said. 'Let me know when she's likely to go on one of these visits and I'll pick it up from there.'

'Good.' He pushed back his chair and stood looking down at the desk for a moment. 'I want all of this kept quiet,' he said finally. 'Nothing of what I've told you and my visit here is to go beyond this office. You understand?'

'I understand perfectly, Mister Jensen.'

'Excellent. When you've got anything, you can contact me on this number.' He handed me a card with a number printed on it.

'You'll be hearing from me,' I said.

He left, closing the door softly as if afraid to let anyone who might be in the building know he'd been.

I sat back in my chair and turned things over in my mind. On the surface, it looked like just another philandering wife straying from the marital bed. A rich man's woman who now got a little bored with life.

Husband working all hours of the day; too much time on her hands and wanting more than just the usual round of parties and social gatherings.

As I'd told him: It happened all the time.

But as they normally did when there was something that didn't quite add up, those little mice had commenced scampering around inside my head.

They were telling me there was something big at the back of all this; something which hadn't come out during my conversation with Jensen.

Maybe, I figured, he did just want to divorce his wife without her getting her pretty hands on a large slice of his dough.

Or maybe he wanted her out of his life on a more permanent basis. What put that idea into my mind, I didn't know. But it was there and it refused to go away.

I decided to go along with him for the time being. But I'd keep my eyes and ears open, just in case there was something more sinister in the offing. In the meantime, I'd dig up whatever I could find on both him and his present wife.

Checking my watch again, I saw that it was well after seven. The library would be closed for the day but the newspaper offices would be open all night. It would soon be time for the graveyard shift to clock on. Maybe I'd strike it lucky and turn up something there.

After parking the Merc in a narrow alley at the side of the block housing the newspaper offices, I went up to the first floor and pushed open the glass door at the end of the corridor. The place smelled of ink and other things I couldn't identify. There were many of the staff around at that time of the evening. Most of the day's news would already be in and being set up on the presses.

I got a few funny looks when I went in but nobody made a move to question me. Maybe they figured I was some hack reporter coming in with a piece of late news for the paper.

I picked on the small, grey-haired guy sitting in the swivel chair behind the nearest desk. He looked as though he might be accommodating and he didn't seem to be too busy.

I showed him my card. He examined it minutely through thick glasses as if it were a valuable piece of jewelry. Then he gave it back.

'What can I do for you, Mister Merak?' he asked, eyeing me up and down.

'I'm looking for some information. I figured this might be the best place to get it.'

'What sort of information?' His eyes narrowed down a shade.

'Background information on one of our most prominent citizens.'

His thick brows went up. 'And who might that be?'

'Charles Henry Jensen III.'

He gave a low whistle through his teeth. Then he studied me again.

Then he closed his eyes and thought. Finally, he opened them again and said, 'What do you want with him? Far as I know, he's squeaky clean. Might even be running for governor one of these days. Why would you be investigating him?'

'I didn't say I was investigating him,' I corrected. 'But it just happens his name's come up in a case I'm working on and I'd like to know a little more about him.'

He paused, then nodded. 'Well, I guess

you're welcome to what we've got. But you're not going to find any dirt on him. I'd say he's one of the straightest guys in L.A.'

'I'm sure he is.'

He eased himself out of the swivel chair, grunting as if the effort made his back hurt. 'How far back do you want to go?'

'Back as far as the divorce from his first wife.'

'That'll be three, no four, years ago. Made big headlines at the time.'

He led the way out of the office and along a narrow side passage.

Each side was stacked high with past editions of the newspaper. Finally, he stopped and pointed. 'There are the ones you want. Help yourself. You can go through them in there.'

He indicated the small office a couple of yards away. It was empty.

After thanking him, I checked through the dates on the papers, then took a pile through. Switching on the small desk lamp, I began skimming through them. I wasn't sure what I was looking for. Maybe nothing. But it was a start.

By the time I'd finished, my vision was beginning to blur. There wasn't much of interest that I didn't already know. But I did come across a couple of items I found intriguing.

Jensen's first wife, Arlene, had apparently disappeared three weeks after the court had granted the divorce. Her sister had reported her missing but after a short investigation, the police had come up with nothing. They'd seemingly reached the conclusion that nothing sinister had occurred. Arlene had taken the money her lawyers had got for her and left the country.

Without any evidence, the police investigation had been closed, despite Arlene's sister's vehement insistence that she would never have left the country without telling her and giving her a forwarding address where she could maintain contact with her.

There was also a report, tucked away in one of the inside pages, relating to two of the top lawyers who had represented Charles Jensen.

Both, it appeared, had been involved in apparently unrelated traffic accidents. Both were victims of hit-and-run drivers and both had been seriously injured. There was no suggestion that these cases were, in any way, connected with the divorce case.

Maybe to anyone else, these events would have seemed nothing more than coincidence. But me — I don't believe in coincidences. I knew right then that I'd have to start digging a lot deeper into this case than I'd originally figured.

I'd read somewhere about those people who'd been instrumental in finding and opening Tutankhamun's tomb in Egypt. Several of them had died because of a so-called curse. If there was any curse associated with Charles Henry Jensen III, I figured it wasn't anything to do with the supernatural.

There was someone in the shadows who was manipulating events. At the moment I had no idea who it was but I sure meant to find out.

I put the newspapers back where I'd got them, thanked the little guy behind the desk for his assistance, and left.

It was now beginning to get dark. The heat was still present in the air. It was a smothering blanket and I decided I needed a drink to cool off. All in all, it had been a pretty exhausting evening.

2

Mancini's bar was open as usual. It wasn't very big, not very jovial, and the glow from the few bulbs gave very little light. Not that that would have helped much. The cigarette smoke which hung in the air, even at that time of night, made it just possible to see the far wall. There was a pool table at the far end with a couple of youths knocking the balls into the pockets.

It was the only sound in the place.

A few early-night customers were already in, two at the bar along the wall to the right. Four others were seated at the round tables that occupied the rest of the bar. You could walk between them if you watched where you put your feet.

One of the guys propping up the bar I didn't know. The other was Sergeant Kolowinski.

In the past, he's always been keen to pass along any information but since I'd nicked his superior, Lieutenant Charles Donovan, for the murder of Carlos Galecci nine months earlier, he'd tried his best to avoid me.

Still, I knew he might be good for some answers if I could get him to talk.

I parked myself on the stool next to his and leaned my elbows on the counter. He didn't look round. I knew he'd recognized me in the glass behind the bar. But for all the attention he paid, the stool next to him might still be empty.

Then, after a minute, he growled, 'I suppose this ain't no social call, Johnny. But if you're looking for any help from me, forget it. I figure you don't have any pals at the precinct now.'

'Somehow, I guessed that.' I ordered a Scotch on the rocks and threw a quick glance around the room. The two youths playing pool weren't bothering anyone. Those at the tables were conversing in low tones, occasionally glancing in my direction. Maybe they knew who I was, maybe they didn't. But it was funny the way they stopped talking the second they knew I was watching them.

'Tell me, Johnny,' This time, Kolowinski turned his head to look at me. 'Why did you bring the Feds in on the Galecci case? Donovan was a damned good cop and Galecci was nothing more than a hoodlum. He deserved all he got.'

I sipped my drink slowly. It helped to clear my head a little.

'Aren't you forgetting Donovan also killed that little old clockmaker who probably never did a wrong thing in his life?'

Kolowinski sighed. 'Maybe he did, maybe he did. But that ain't the way most of the boys in the precinct see it.'

'All right,' I said. 'Why argue? I was only doing my job as you do yours. If you don't want to help me, fair enough.'

There was a long pause. I knew he was interested. I could almost hear the tiny cog wheels grinding away inside his head.

Then he drained his glass and set it down on the counter. It was placed right up to mine. I took the hint. Signalling to the barkeep, I told him to fill it up again.

'Okay, Johnny. Maybe I'm being plain stupid. What is it this time?'

I took out a cigarette and lit it before offering him one. He shook his head sorrowfully. 'I'm trying to give it up,' he said. From the expression on his face I gathered it was a self-inflicted penance and one he could do without.

'What do you know about Arlene Jensen? According to the newspapers of the time, she vanished just after Charles Jensen divorced her.'

'Can't say I know much about that.' He shook his head. If my question surprised him, he didn't show it.

'You should if you read any of your own reports.' I told him. 'You were one of the investigating officers when her sister reported her missing.'

'Hell, Johnny. We get missing persons reports come into the precinct every day of the week. Most of 'em are just runaway husbands or wives. You can't expect me to remember details of every one.'

'You should remember this one. High society dame. Husband a multi-millionaire, head of the Jensen Construction Corporation. You don't get many like that.'

He tossed half of his drink down in a

single gulp. 'Okay, I remember it now. But hell — that was nearly four years ago. Besides, there was no evidence that anything had happened to the dame. My guess is she just took the alimony and skipped the country. Maybe she figured her husband could make a lot more trouble for her if she stuck around too long.'

'You got any ideas where she could've gone?'

His lips tightened into a hard line. 'Nope. No idea at all. Far as we were concerned, no criminal act had been committed and she was free to go anywhere she liked.'

'Was her sister satisfied with that?'

'I guess so. We never heard any more about it.'

'All right,' I said. 'We'll let that drop. Now for another question.'

'Hellfire, Johnny. Don't you ever stop asking questions?'

'Not while I've got unanswered questions running around inside my head. They keep me awake at nights.' I blew a cloud of smoke into the already thick air.

'What more do you want to know?'

'Those two high-flying lawyers who represented Charles Jensen. Seems they both met with accidents just around the time that Arlene disappeared. Were they accidents? Or was somebody out to get them?'

His glass was now empty again and I waited patiently while the bartender poured another shot into it. He sat staring at it for a while like a puppy that had just found its bone.

Then he cleared his throat and nodded. His tone was now more serious than before. 'You've always played square with me in the past, Johnny, so I guess I owe you one. But what I'm going to tell you now goes no further than this bar, understand? If anything gets out, I'll deny I ever talked to you.'

'Go on.'

'I remember everything about those two cases. Not just because they seemed more than just coincidence, those two guys getting hurt — but because it was all hushed up, closed up tighter than the Hoover dam. There was just that little piece that got into the papers.

'But it seems they both received threatening mail when it became known they were acting for Charles Jensen. He was doing his damnedest to make sure she never got a cent. Most of the evidence that was given to prove her adultery was cooked up and so full of holes you could've strained soup through it.

'Whoever it was ran them down within a week of each other was never identified. They were both lucky not to have been killed — if you can call it lucky. One of 'em is in some private sanitorium outside the state with permanent brain damage. The other guy was in hospital for months and they reckon he'll never walk again.'

'You figure it was the same guy who ran down both of them?'

'We were damned sure it was the same person. There just happened to be an eyewitness to the second incident. We got the make of the car and most of the registration number.'

'Let me guess,' I butted in. 'It was Charles Jensen's car.'

He shook his head. 'Nice try, Johnny,

but you're wrong. The car belonged to Arlene Jensen. Her husband gave it her just after they were married. And it was a woman driving it.'

'Arlene Jensen?' I tried to figure that one out, but I couldn't. Even if she'd been mad enough to harbour a grudge against those who gave cooked-up evidence against her, she wasn't likely to kill them. 'Didn't you try to find her and bring her in for questioning?'

'Sure. But before we could put out any feelers, word came down from the top that no charges had been made by either of those guys and the case was closed. We were to forget it. To me, it looked like attempted murder. But there was nothing we could do.'

He gave me a funny kind of smile. 'And don't waste your time trying to get your hands on the case files. Funnily enough, they both went missing some time ago.'

'That doesn't surprise me at all. The big question is — who put the clamps on it?'

Kolowinski shrugged his shoulders. 'Your guess is as good as mine. But it must have been someone pretty big. I'd advise you to watch your back if you've taken this case. It's all right raking up the dirt from the past. But if that someone is still around, you could find yourself up to your neck in big trouble.'

'Thanks, I'll keep that in mind.'

I got up and went out into the night. There was the faint smell of the desert in the air, hot and dry. It sometimes came over like that when the wind was in the right quarter.

I decided to walk for a while before driving back to my apartment and turning in for the night. I'd got some answers but they weren't the ones I wanted and they didn't make any sense. It was just possible the walk would clear my head a little.

What had I got so far? Charles Jensen had walked into my office and asked me to follow his wayward wife. A straight-forward case if there ever was one. Or so it had seemed.

Now, after only a couple of hours' digging, it seemed to have turned into something much bigger. An unexplained disappearance. Two hit-and-run accidents that were almost certainly related attempted murders. A woman driver who could have been the missing Arlene Jensen.

As Shakespeare once said: Something stank.

I'd walked for about half a mile in the direction of the bay, turning things over in my mind. There was a hot-dog stand just across the street. The guy there was wearing an apron that had once been as white as the driven snow. Now it was a greasy grey. The sight, however, reminded me I'd not eaten since midday.

There were a couple of customers waiting while he stabbed the weinies with his fork, placed them with an exaggerated care between the cut rolls, and squeezed a generous helping of mustard along each.

I bought one when my turn came and moved quickly out of the way as a couple of sailors with laughing girls on their arms moved up behind me. The hotdog lived up to its name. It was hot and the mustard burned my tongue but at least it tasted good.

I was halfway through it when someone

moved out of the shadows and sidled up to me. He had a milk-white face that looked as if it had been out of the sun for far too long. A battered hat almost covered his eyes.

I had him figured for a bum on the take.

The corner of his mouth twitched. 'Drop the case, Merak,' he muttered. 'This is just a friendly warning. If you don't, the next time things won't be quite so friendly.'

'Hey,' I said. I reached out my free hand to grab his arm. I wasn't used to being threatened like that. Not by total strangers while I was eating, anyway.

He was quick, but not fast enough. My hand closed around his wrist like a clamp as he tried to slip away. His other hand went up to his coat. Maybe he was just getting out a handkerchief but I was taking no chances. Before his hand could reach his lapel, I'd let him go and I had the .38 out and clicked off the safety catch loudly enough for him to hear.

If his face could have turned any whiter, I'm sure it would. 'Just move back a little,' I said evenly.

He did as he was told.

'This won't get you a thing,' he stammered.

'We'll just have to see about that,' I said. 'I don't know you, but you seem to know me. Who told you to give me that message?'

Out of the corner of my eye, I saw one of the sailors give me a funny look. Maybe he reckoned it was a shakedown. For a moment, I thought he was going to come over. Then he must have decided it was none of his business and turned back to the cutie by his side.

'I — I don't know who she was, mister — ' The little guy was almost whining now. ' — All I know is I'm walking past Mancini's when this car drives up and stops alongside me. The window goes down and this dame calls me over. She points you out to me as you come out of the bar and tells me to follow you and see that you get the message. Then she slips me a twenty and drives off.'

I put the safety catch back on. His story

sounded too fantastic to be anything but the truth.

'Can you describe this dame?' I asked.

'Sure. A real looker. Long black hair, grey eyes. She must have plenty of dough to be driving around in a car like that.'

'But you've no idea who she is?'

He shook his head. 'Never seen her before. Honest to God, mister.'

'Okay.' I put the gun away. 'You've delivered your message.'

He stood for a minute rubbing his wrist. Then he moved off into the small crowd hanging around the stall.

I watched him until he disappeared. So far, the night had proved interesting. But I didn't like the way things were shaping up.

I finished my hot dog and then walked back to where I'd left the car. Sitting behind the wheel, I took out the photograph Jensen had given me. The description the little guy had given me certainly didn't fit Janine Jensen. But there was one other possibility. It might fit Arlene but unless she was still around, keeping out of sight, I couldn't see how she could possibly have known Jensen had been to see me.

I figured I needed to get a picture of Arlene. First thing in the morning. I'd check through the newspapers again. After the way his first marriage had broken up, I reckoned Charles Jensen would be the last person in the world who'd want to keep a photograph of Arlene.

Swinging the Merc out of the side street, I turned into the main stream of traffic. Had I not been checking my side mirror, I guess I would have missed the car that pulled away from the kerb twenty yards behind. Maybe there was nothing to it, I thought, but half a block further on, I made a sharp right.

The street ahead of me was empty apart from a couple of saloons parked at the side. I drove on for a further fifty yards, then pulled in to the right, switching oft the lights. A couple of seconds later, bright headlights showed and the Chrysler I'd noticed turned the corner.

Whoever was driving it must have

30

spotted the Merc right away and figured out what I'd done. The Chrysler stopped immediately.

Very gently, I eased the .38 from its holster, opened the door and slipped out, crouching down beside the car. The nearest streetlamp was about fifteen yards in front of the Chrysler and the light was reflected from the windscreen so that it was impossible to make out any details of the driver.

I could hear the engine purring away like a contented cat. Then, suddenly, the car leapt forward. Something warned me that whoever was behind the wheel of that car hadn't just realized they were late for a party. I pulled my head down as far as it would go. The next second something smashed through the side window of the Merc, just above my skull. I heard it hit the wall of the building beside me and go screeching off into the night.

There had been no sound of a shot. I guessed whoever it was had used a silencer and reckoned I was still sitting behind the wheel awaiting events. Pushing myself up I was just in time to see the taillights vanishing around the far corner.

Back in my apartment, I phoned the precinct to report this incident. I got the desk sergeant who gave his name as McNaughton. When I gave him my name, his tone became frosty.

'Okay, Mister Merak,' he said icily. 'Can you give me a description of the car?'

'Sure. A dark blue Chrysler.'

I knew from his tone that he'd heard of me. Possibly he'd once been a good pal of Lieutenant Donovan's.

'Did you get the registration?'

'Hell no. It was too dark and everything happened so fast.'

I could picture him standing behind the desk trying to figure out how he could put the phone down without giving me cause to report him. I doubted if he was writing anything down.

'You say there was one shot fired at your car by someone using a silencer? Were there any witnesses?'

'None that I could see.'

'All right, Mister Merak. I'll put in a report but I suppose you know how many blue Chryslers there are in L.A.'

'About as many as there are cops,' I said nastily and put the phone down. I knew I'd get no help from them.

I looked at the whiskey bottle on the table, felt tempted for a moment, then decided against it. Crawling into bed, I switched off the light and lay listening to the sound of the late night traffic. Things were happening a little too fast for my liking. It was clear that someone didn't want me probing into the events immediately following Jensen's first divorce.

Maybe if I'd asked that little, white-faced guy for a description of the car the woman had been driving as well as that of the dame driving it, I might be in a position to connect the two. At the moment, I only had a hunch they were one and the same person. Maybe she had me figured as someone who couldn't take a hint and had decided to take me out of the picture permanently before I could dig up any more dirt.

3

Dawn was already in the office when I walked in the next morning. She flashed me a brief smile that didn't last long before a concerned expression crossed her face.

'My God, Johnny, you look awful.'

'I didn't have a very good night,' I said. 'Too many things running through my mind.'

'I'll make you some coffee, strong and black.' She got up. 'You look as though you need it.'

'Thanks.' I waited until it came, then sipped it slowly. It burned my throat, but it helped.

She sat down in the chair opposite and rested her elbows on the desk. 'Want to tell me about it?'

Briefly, I described the events of the previous evening. She listened without interrupting once until I'd finished.

Then she said gravely, 'You think that

whoever tried to kill you was the same woman who got that man to give you a warning to drop the Jensen case?'

'It's the only thing that makes any kind of sense,' I admitted. 'I'm not sure whether that slug was meant to put me permanently off the case or just to reinforce the warning. But from what the guy said it couldn't have been Janine Jensen. Yet she's the only one who could somehow have known he was coming here.'

'Have you told the police?' Dawn asked.

I nodded. 'Sure. But somehow I doubt if they'll do anything about it. Ever since I got Lieutenant Donovan arrested for Galecci's murder, my name there is mud. Maybe they're even sorry that slug didn't find its mark last night.'

'So much for our impartial police force. So what do you intend doing now? You still mean to go ahead with Jensen?'

'Of course. There's no reason to turn down a five thousand dollar retainer. This case is proving a lot more interesting than I thought and I have the feeling that — '

'Interesting?' Dawn's eyes narrowed

down at the corners. 'I'd say it's getting more deadly by the minute.'

At that moment, the phone on the desk shrilled. I picked it up, expecting it to be Charles Jensen letting me know his wife was about to set off on another of her weekend jaunts.

It wasn't. Instead, a man's voice I didn't recognize, said, 'Is that Mister Merak?'

'That's the name.'

'Miss Barbara Winton would like to see you as soon as possible.'

'Barbara Winton?' I said. I looked across the desk at Dawn. She shook her head slowly. 'I'm afraid I don't know the name. Perhaps if she was to tell me what this is all about, I — '

'You know the name Arlene Jensen,' said the voice. 'Miss Winton is her sister.'

'I see,' I said. I didn't, but I decided to play along with this until I knew what was going on. 'And where would she like to meet?'

I had the feeling that things were happening far too quickly for my liking, one event crowding on another without any pause in between.

'Do you know the *Drayton Hotel* in Bay City?'

'Who doesn't?' I replied. The *Drayton* was arguably the biggest and most expensive hotel along the bay. Most of the stars and film directors stayed there whenever they were in town.

'Room 224. Half an hour. You'll be expected.'

There was a click and the line went dead. I put the receiver down and sat looking at the phone as if expecting to see the answers to all this engraved on the smooth plastic.

'Well?' Dawn said. 'What did Miss Barbara Winton want?'

'That wasn't her,' I said. 'Could have been the butler but I figure it was more likely some hired gorilla looking after her interests. It seems she's Arlene Jensen's sister.'

Dawn looked suitably surprised. 'You think she may know something about Arlene?'

'There's only one way to find out.' I got up.

'You could be walking into big trouble here, Johnny.'

'I know. But that's a risk you sometimes have to take in this business. In the meantime, you can do something for me. I need a picture of Arlene. You'll probably find one in the newspapers around the time of the divorce. It made headline news.'

I checked the .38 was still nestling in its holster, then grabbed my hat and made for the door. Behind me, Dawn called, 'Watch yourself. Remember Gloria Galecci.'

I remembered. The last big case I'd had. Carlos Galecci's wife. A stunning six-foot blonde with a killer instinct.

Bay City was hot and dusty but fortunately there wasn't too much traffic around and I found a parking space close to the *Drayton Hotel*. A man in a monkey suit stood just outside the imposing doors. He stepped forward as I made to enter.

'Are you registered here, sir?' The tone of his voice implied that he knew I wasn't and that unless I had a very good reason, he wasn't going to allow me in.

'No,' I said. 'But I am expected by

someone who is.'

His thick brows went up until they almost vanished inside the hairline under his hat.

'Barbara Winton,' I went on evenly. 'I believe she's in Room 224. You can check if you like. The name's Merak.'

'Wait here.' He turned and walked through the swing doors. I could just see him making his way to the desk.

When he came back a few minutes later, there was a different expression on his face and his general attitude had changed completely.

'Miss Winton is expecting you, Mister Merak,' he said and there was an almost servile edge to his tone. He obviously didn't like me, didn't believe that such people as myself should be allowed into the hotel. But he'd clearly received his orders and there was nothing he could do about it.

'Thanks,' I said. 'I'll be sure to let Miss Winton know how good the service is here.'

The glare he gave me almost made the air sizzle.

Going inside, I got into the elevator and pushed the button for the second floor. I guess it must have moved but I didn't feel a thing. The door slid open and I stepped out into a long corridor with a plush red carpet along the middle of it. All of the doors on either side were closed but there was one about halfway along the corridor to my left that had a guy sitting in a chair beside it. He was reading a newspaper and didn't even look up as I walked towards him.

There wasn't a sound. For all the noise I made, I might have been a shadow.

Even when the big guy stood up, it was as quiet as if every bone and joint in his body had just been oiled.

'You Merak, the private dick?' His voice was like rocks tumbling down a chute.

'That's right,' I said. 'I believe Miss Winton is expecting me.'

He folded his newspaper with an exaggerated care, then knocked softly on the door. It opened and an even bigger guy stood there, eyeing me up and down. My friend from outside said something and the other guy stood on one side and waved me to go in. Neither guy checked me for the .38.

It was a cosy room. Two big Grecian urns stood on pedestals on either side of the door and on the floor was a carpet straight out of the Arabian Nights. I expected it to rise up and waft me straight out of the window.

The furnishings were exquisite. It was so clearly done out as a woman's room that the big guy standing beside me looked distinctly out of place.

Apart from us, there were two other people in the room. One was a tall, sharp-faced man with steely eyes, dressed in a sombre brown suit.

The other was a slim woman of around thirty-five. She was wearing a dark navy suit with a low-necked pale-blue blouse. Her eyes were of the most piercing blue I had ever seen and I guessed that if she got real angry, those eyes could bore right through you like a drill.

Her hair was that jet black which shone, falling in waves to her shoulders. The only jewelry she wore was a diamond pendant around her neck and one of those charm bracelets you sometimes see on society dames around her left wrist.

She was seated on a low leather divan, her elegant legs crossed seemingly carelessly. But I knew she was that kind of woman who knew exactly what kind of effect she was having on anyone in her vicinity.

She motioned to one of the chairs at either end of the divan. 'Would you like a drink, Mister Merak?' she asked.

I glanced deliberately at my watch. I didn't want her to think I was one of those private eyes who hit the bottle every hour of the day.

She glanced at the big man standing patiently near the door. 'Get Mister Merak a drink, honey,' she said. 'Bourbon and ice.'

I nodded. 'That will be fine,' I said.

The guy went to the drinks cabinet in one corner of the room, came back with the drink and handed it to me.

While I sipped it appreciatively, she said, 'You already know that Arlene was my sister and it's imperative I talk to you.'

'Why do you say Arlene *was* your

sister? Do you have any concrete proof she's no longer alive?'

Before replying, she took out a slim gold cigarette case, extracting a cigarette and lighting it with a silver lighter. Blowing smoke delicately into the air, she said, 'That's the main reason why I asked you here.'

'If this has anything to do directly with Charles Jensen, I can't take your case.'

'Just listen to what I have to say, that's all I'm asking at the moment.'

I sighed. 'Very well, I'm listening.'

She settled herself more demurely on the divan. 'I've never believed she left the country as the police maintain. Indeed, I don't believe she ever left Bay City.'

'I can understand your concern,' I said. 'But if you've got me here to look for her, dead or alive, it's out of the question. I have another important case which is taking up all of my time.'

She studied me with those eyes for almost a full minute, making me feel uncomfortable. I had the feeling she was trying to make some kind of decision,

43

possibly wondering how far I could be trusted.

Then she eased her shoulders back and said, 'You feel you can't accept me as a client because it would conflict with what you have in hand for Charles Jensen.'

I sat up straight at that. I could feel those little mice beginning to stir inside my mind. I felt suddenly stiff. I thought hard but I couldn't figure out how she could possibly have known about that.

Certainly she'd never got that information from Jensen himself and unless she was in cahoots with Janine, which seemed highly unlikely.

As if reading my mind, she went on, 'I can see you're wondering about that.' She smiled faintly, just a curve of the lips, nothing more. 'It's quite simple. Ever since my sister vanished, I've employed my own private investigator to keep tags on Charles Jensen. I know almost every move he makes, day or night.'

'Then why ask me here if you've already got someone on your case?'

She leaned forward and moved the fingers of one well-manicured hand around the rim of her glass. 'Firstly, because he's got a full-time job on his hands keeping an eye on Jensen.'

'And secondly — ?'

'I know something of your reputation, Mister Merak. And what I've heard, I like.'

'All right,' I growled. I downed half of my drink. The big guy certainly knew how to mix a bourbon with just the right amount of ice. 'You like the way I work. But that doesn't alter the fact I'm still working for Jensen.'

She glanced up at the dapper guy hovering soundlessly in the background. 'This is Phil Denson, my lawyer, by the way. What do you say to that, Phil?'

Denson shrugged. 'It's definitely not ethical. There could be a conflict of interests here and — '

Barbara held up a hand. She looked directly at me. 'I won't tell if you don't.'

'That isn't the point,' I replied. 'I could quite easily have my licence revoked. The cops aren't exactly pleased with me at the moment.'

'All right,' she said obliquely. 'Let's try

this one. I'm quite certain Arlene is dead — and that Charles Jensen had her killed.'

I sat up at that. I had to admit there'd been a nagging little suspicion flitting around inside my head for some time but I hadn't taken much notice of it.

'Why would Charles Jensen want Arlene killed? Sure, it wasn't an amicable divorce and she got a hell of a lot more of his dough than he'd have liked. But that isn't a strong enough motive for having her killed.'

She stubbed out her cigarette in the ashtray. I noticed her hand was trembling slightly.

'Maybe that's the way you and the police see it. But there is another motive.'

I was beginning to get interested. 'Go on.'

She motioned to the bruiser and he came and refilled my glass. 'I don't normally drink as early in the day as this,' I said.

'Of course.' Her smile was broader this time. It seemed a little more relaxed, more friendly. Then she sobered instantly.

'Arlene was no dumbhead even though her husband and his friends always thought she was. He used to take her down a lot in front of their guests. But she knew a lot of what was going on in his business although she was wise enough to keep her mouth shut.'

'You think she was murdered because she knew too much?'

She considered that for a moment, then gave a brief nod. 'Believe me, Mister Merak, if Arlene had told everything she knew to the Feds, Charles Jensen would now be in jail along with all those other hoodlums he was working with.'

I drank down half my drink. A few of the little bits of the jigsaw were now beginning to slot into place and I didn't like the picture that was emerging. I didn't doubt she was telling the truth. It merely confirmed some of the suspicions I'd had from the moment Charles Jensen had walked out of my office.

'Did your sister tell you any of this?' I asked.

'Some. But it was enough.'

'And you realize that if Jensen should

learn any of this, your life wouldn't be worth a plugged nickel, assuming that what you've told me is true.'

'Of course I realize it,' she said. Her voice was quiet and acid at the same time. 'And so do you. Why do you think I have men guarding me all the time I'm here?'

She lit another cigarette and watched me finish my drink.

I put the glass down and asked, 'Do you own a dark blue Chrysler?'

Her eyes widened in what looked like genuine surprise. 'No — why?'

'Just a thought.'

'That's a funny kind of thought,' she said. 'But if you really want to know, I own a red Mercedes. You'll probably notice it in the car park when you leave.'

I said nothing.

Assuming a business-like tone, she continued, 'Having told you everything about Charles Jensen, do you still feel it's unethical to take my case as well? I don't expect you to divulge anything about him that doesn't directly concern my sister's disappearance.'

'And this other investigator you've

hired — I presume he'll still stick with that side of the investigation?'

'Of course. Is that a problem?'

I shook my head. 'No problem. Just so long as we don't get our wires crossed.'

She ran that over in her mind for a moment, then gave a brief smile and got elegantly to her feet. 'When can I expect to hear from you?'

'It'll take a little time. Like I said, I'm still retained by Mister Jensen. But I promise I'll look into what might have happened to your sister.'

'Thank you.' She paused, waiting to see if I meant to say anything further. When I didn't, she said, 'I'll be staying here for another week. After that, I'll be going back home.' She motioned to Denson who dug into his inside pocket and came up with a card. 'That's my home address and phone number. You can reach me there in a week's time.'

I took the card. It was one of those expensive printed ones with an address in San Francisco. I placed it carefully in my wallet.

The big guy held the door open for me

as I left. In the corridor, the other minder was still reading his newspaper. I figured if I came back in two days' time he would still be reading the same page.

I got back to the office twenty minutes later. Dawn was already there.

'Did you have a cosy little chat with Miss Winton?' she asked. 'I gather she offered you a drink.'

'Nothing like a drink to get people to talk,' I said smoothly. 'Did you manage to get a picture of Arlene Jensen?'

She held it out to me. It was a photocopy obviously taken from an old newspaper. It had apparently been taken some five years before around the time she was married to Jensen.

It wasn't a perfect picture, a little smudged around the edges, but it showed an attractive brunette and there was a definite resemblance to Barbara Winton. There was, however, a certain hardness about the features and the determined set of the jaw told me that, like Jensen's present wife, Janine, here was a woman who was resolved to have her own way.

I could believe that Jensen's description

of her as a gold-digger hadn't been far short of the mark. I had to give the guy that. And if she had, by some means, managed to dig up some dirt on him and his business associates, she'd put that information to good use. But the face in the picture also told me she was a very careful woman who didn't do things on impulse.

She'd consider all of the ramifications of her actions first, knowing that if she was right, the people her husband was tied in with would stop at nothing to protect their interests. Even to the point of making sure she couldn't spill anything she knew to the authorities. More and more, I was coming round to Barbara Winton's belief that her sister had been murdered.

So where did that leave me as far as Charles Jensen was concerned? I reached for the pack of cigarettes on the desk. My hand was halfway there when the thought hit me. It was a thought that came right out of the blue without any warning.

'So that's why he's so desperate to find

out who she's seeing.'

'Who's so desperate?' Dawn asked.

I hadn't realized I'd spoken my thoughts out aloud. 'Charles Jensen, of course. He doesn't want me to follow Janine just to get evidence of her adultery. Barbara Winton believes her sister is dead, that she was murdered and Jensen was behind it.'

'Because he had to pay out all that alimony and his ego couldn't accept it?' Dawn sounded dubious.

'Hell — no. Because, somehow, she found out he's working with a bunch of hoodlums, the big men behind the Mob. That would have finished him completely.'

Dawn bit her lower lip, then said, 'So you think Janine also knows about these shady deals and he's scared she's about to tell?'

'It makes sense.'

'So who's the mystery woman in the blue Chrysler who warned you off the case and is trying to kill you?'

'That,' I said, 'is something I'm trying to figure out. I guess we can eliminate

Arlene Jensen and her sister. That leaves only Janine.'

'I don't get it. Unless she knew her husband was here and she's scared you might give him sufficient ammunition to want to kill her. Besides, there's just one thing you haven't considered.'

'What's that?'

'Maybe Arlene is still alive in spite of what her sister thinks. Even though she did get that alimony, she might have been pretty sore at those lawyers who acted for her ex-husband, particularly the dirt they tried to drag up against her, sore enough to try to kill them. It's been four years. You'd think if she was dead, they'd have found a body by now.'

'Only if they were looking for one. The police weren't. That case was closed on orders from someone pretty high up.'

'So you're going to open it up again?'

'I'm seriously thinking about it,' I told her.

'That means you are. Sometimes I think you do these things for the sheer hell of it, not for the money.'

I said nothing. Sometimes she was right.

After a few moments, she said, 'How are you going to start? I mean, if she was killed by the time her sister reported her missing, any trail there was will now be as cold as Spitzbergen in winter.'

'I still have a few contacts,' I said. 'Maybe one of them can come up with something.'

4

That evening I drove out of L.A. towards the hills north of Bay City. I'd made a telephone call that afternoon and the guy I spoke to had agreed to meet me at a spot well off the coast highway. His name was Tony Ricardo. Some years before, I'd managed to get him off the hook for carrying marihuana and he still owed me a favour.

He wasn't the type who liked to be seen talking with private investigators. It not only spoiled his image but some of his colleagues in the Mob might get the wrong idea and he could end up on the bottom of the bay with concrete strapped to his ankles.

Dawn hadn't liked the idea of me meeting him in such an isolated spot. Just to please her I carried the .38 under my left arm.

There was still plenty of traffic on the highway and the fog was starting to come down. Even at that time of the year it seemed to drift down from the hills. I cut my speed as the light from the headlights was thrown back at me so that, at times, it was as if I was driving through a blanket.

I wasn't particularly well acquainted with this part of the country but Ricardo had given me explicit directions. Once I turned off the highway and up into the hills, it got very quiet. A couple of big trucks crawled up the side of the hill in front of me. If the drivers had figured they could make better time making a detour off the highway, they'd made a big mistake.

The fog was thicker here than down below, forcing them to a crawl. Then they would accelerate on the downgrade making it impossible for me to overtake before the next rise loomed up. I checked the luminous face of my watch. Knowing Tony, he'd perhaps wait for five, maybe ten, minutes and then leave.

Peering through the windscreen, I put the wipers on to clear the fog from the glass. The headlights went so far into the fog, then gave up the struggle. Drive over three rises and then take the turn to the right, Ricardo had told me. Topping the third rise, I tried to make out what lay in front of me.

I was right on top of the turning before I realized it. Cursing under my breath, I swung the Merc off the road. Now I was driving on what probably passed as a road in this backwater area. Parts of it were missing and here and there, some super weed had forced its way through narrow cracks. I'd seen better roads in some of the old Western movies.

In places there were buildings along each side but no lights showed and I guessed that whoever had once lived there had figured any other place had to be better than this and had moved out long ago. The road ended and in front of me was nothing but sage and brush.

I stopped the car and got out, leaving the engine running and the headlights on. Ragged boulders dotted the slope in front of me and I didn't want to risk breaking my ankle in the fog and darkness.

Around me the silence was like the inside of a coffin. Nothing moved. After a few minutes, I figured that the delay in sticking behind those freights on the hill road had been long enough for Ricardo to have given up waiting.

Then a sound froze me to the spot.

A faint rustle in the sage off to my left. I managed to spin round without jumping a foot into the air. The .38 was already in my hand. Then a figure loomed blackly out of the drifting fog.

'That you, Johnny?'

Even though it had been almost a year I recognized Ricardo's voice at once and lowered the gun slowly.

'Yes,' I answered.

He came closer, a little guy with a wide-brimmed hat pulled down well over his eyes. 'You sure you weren't followed?'

'Quite sure.' I slipped the gun back into its holster.

'Okay. You said you were looking for information.' He pushed a cigarette between his lips, sparked a match, and lit it. 'What kind of information?'

'I'm currently working on a case — actually two cases,' I told him. 'Both concern Charles Jensen.'

He whistled thinly through his teeth. 'You're up in the big league there, Johnny. Better watch you don't get your fingers burned. That guy could do you a lot of harm if you're not careful.'

'So I've been told.' I didn't say anything more for a minute. Then I said, 'I'm trying to find out what happened to his first wife, Arlene. Some folk reckon she's skipped the country. Others figure she's dead.'

'Arlene Jensen.' He seemed to be turning the name over in his mind.

I guessed it was a name he hadn't expected.

'You know a lot more of what goes on in the Mobs, Tony. You must have heard something — even if it's only rumours.'

I thought he shrugged but in the darkness I couldn't be sure.

'There was talk that she knew too much for her own good,' he said finally. 'I guess you already know Jensen's been mixed up in some pretty shady deals.'

'So people have told me. And I know that someone tried to kill a couple of

59

smart lawyers Jenson hired for his divorce.'

'You seem to know quite a lot,' he remarked dryly.

'Yeah, but not enough by a long way. That's why I'm hoping you can tell me a bit more.'

'Just what's your interest in Arlene Jensen?'

'Her sister has hired me to find out what happened to her. She's pretty sure she was murdered and Jensen was behind it.'

'If he was, I'm darned sure you'll never be able to prove it.'

'She is dead then?'

He uttered a low, throaty laugh. 'I didn't say that — you did.' Then he went on more seriously. 'Her sister's right in one detail. There was a hit put out on Arlene Jensen. I've no idea who did it. But there was big money involved.'

'So it could have been her ex-husband?'

'Could've been,' he agreed. 'Funny thing, though, I never heard whether the hit was carried out.'

'Did you know her at all?' I asked.

'Met her a couple of times. Big functions that Jensen supported. Legit on the surface but some of the guys who attended were from the Mob. Not that you'd have known, of course.'

'What was your impression of her?'

'High-class dame. But not your usual run of society dames. Arlene was a shrewd cookie although she went to a lot of trouble not to show it. If she knew anything, she wouldn't hesitate to blackmail Jensen once he showed signs of getting tired of her and started looking for a divorce. She was as cold as ice inside.'

'You mean she'd threaten to spill everything, knowing she'd be taking on the Mob if she did.'

He nodded. 'She'd have made her plans before she did anything. I figure she also had friends, influential friends, who could help her disappear off the face of the earth before the Mob could get to her.'

'But you've no idea who those influential friends might be?'

He thought hard for a moment before replying. 'There was one guy, a big oil magnate from Texas. Rumour had it he was real sweet on her before she met up with Jensen. There was talk she was engaged to him for a time but she broke it off and married Jensen.'

'You know his name?'

'Sure, Clem Belvedere. The engagement would be in one of those society magazines of the time if you want to check.'

'I'll check.' I said. 'Is there anything more you can tell me?'

'There's one other lead you might want to follow up.' He dug inside his jacket pocket. There was the rustle of paper. He thrust it into my hand. 'This cop worked on the case of those two lawyers who were run down just after the divorce case. I guess he opened his mouth a little too much when it was closed on orders from the top.'

I struck a match and glanced at the name on the paper. 'Joe Kerman.' I said almost in a whisper. 'What about him?'

'By all accounts, he was an honest cop, wanted desperately to keep the case open. Even went so far as to accuse the Police

Commissioner of a cover-up. Said neither of the two lawyers were in any fit state to stop any charges being brought.'

'That wouldn't go down too well at the precinct.'

'It didn't. They kicked him out of the force on some trumped up charge. If you can get him when he's half sober, you might get something important out of him.'

'And where might I find him?'

'His home is usually The Oyster Bar on Main Street.'

'Thanks.' I pushed a tenspot into his hand. 'If you do learn anything more, you know where to find me.'

'Sure.' I saw him thrust the bill into his pocket. Then he drifted away into the fog and became less and less substantial until he disappeared.

I walked back to the Merc. I hadn't asked Ricardo how he'd got there. I reckoned he had a car stashed somewhere out of sight. He certainly hadn't walked all the way from town.

I figured that everything he'd told me was the truth as far as he knew it. There was no point in him lying about anything. If the Mob ever found out he'd spoken to me he wouldn't last another day. If it wasn't the bay, someone would stumble across him in an alley and he'd become just another statistic.

By the time I hit Main Street, the fog in town had cleared. My throat was feeling like the middle of the Sahara on a hot day and I needed a drink. The bars were still open and I figured the best place to get one was The Oyster. From what Ricardo had told me, this ex-cop Kerman was as sure to be there as Sunday followed Saturday.

Whether I'd get anything out of him, drunk or half-sober, was in the lap of the gods. But it was worth a try.

Parking the Merc a few yards from the bar, I went inside, under the big red neon sign above the swing doors. The place was very different to Mancini's. All spinning lights and noise. Half of L.A. seemed to be packed inside the place.

I pushed my way through the crowd until I reached the end of the bar. There were five guys serving the drinks and each of them seemed to be busy. Finally, I attracted the attention of one of them; a youngish fellow in a white shirt and dark-colored trousers.

'What'll it be?' he asked.

'Bourbon on the rocks,' I said.

He brought it a minute later and set it down in front of me. As he made to move away, I said, 'Do you know a customer named Kerman? Used to be a cop.'

His face suddenly took on a stony look. 'Who wants to know?'

'His fairy godmother,' I said. I took out my card and pushed it across the counter, making sure he caught a glimpse of the .38 in the holster.

He picked it up, studied it for a moment, then handed it back. 'Are you working with the cops?'

I shook my head. 'No. Like it says there. I'm a private investigator. I'd just like to talk to Joe Kerman.'

He grinned as if what I'd said was a big joke. 'Knowing Kerman, I'll lay odds he won't want to talk to you.'

'I thought of that. But maybe when he hears who I am, he'll change his mind.'

He ran this over in his mind, then lifted the flap at the end of the bar and came out. He moved lazily in front of me, working his way through the crowd and the smoke.

We went to the far corner of the room. There was a table there and just one guy sitting at it — or rather he was slumped across it with his head resting on one arm. There was a half-empty whisky glass in front of him.

The barkeep shook him nervously by the shoulder. 'Someone here wants to see you, Joe.'

'Huh?' The head lifted and Kerman stared up at me.

'You're Joe Kerman?'

'So what?'

'I think you can give me the answers to some questions.'

With an effort, he pushed himself off the table and slumped back in his chair. There was a look in his eyes which suggested that, drunk or not, he could still start trouble.

'I don't talk to no cops.' He rubbed the back of his hand across his mouth. Then he glanced at the liquor, made as if to pick it up, then pushed it away.

'I know you don't,' I said. 'And I know why.'

He looked at me for quite a long time before he said, 'Just who are you?'

'The name's Merak, private investigator.'

Something came into his eyes at that. The drink had got to his brain and it wasn't working as fast as in his younger days. Then the name clicked. He stared up at the barkeep still hovering like a butterfly at my back. A pause, then the young guy melted away like a wisp of fog.

'You're the guy who nailed Donovan.'

'That's right. And for doing my public duty, I'm not too well liked by the cops.'

'Donovan was the guy who got me busted four years ago.' His lips curled. 'For doing my public duty.'

'He won't be busting any more honest cops where he is,' I said. 'I figure you owe me something for that.'

Kerman's hand reached for the glass. His fingers curled around it but he didn't lift it. Somehow, I'd got through to him, reached that spark of righteous anger in his mind. He seemed to have sobered appreciably within ten seconds.

'All right,' he said. His voice dropped a decibel lower. 'So you're Johnny Merak. What do you want?'

'I want to know everything you found out about those two lawyers who acted for Charles Jensen four years ago — and also who put the clamps on the case. Not Donovan — Mister Big at the top.'

'Giving out information like that could be dangerous, even if I knew it.'

'You know it. What surprises me is that you didn't take it to City Hall at the time.'

His teeth showed in a wolfish grin at that remark. 'You think I'd go to them? Sure I was mad at the time, mad enough to do almost anything, but I'm not stupid. I'd be looking up at the fishes from the bottom of the Bay. Half the guys in City Hall wouldn't believe me and the other half were in on it.'

I took out a cigarette, offered him one. We both lit up. I sipped my drink but Kerman didn't touch his.

'Anything you can tell me stays in here — ' I tapped the side of my head. ' — nothing on paper, not a word to anyone else.'

He reflected on that for a few seconds, then nodded. 'All right, I'll trust you, Merak. Like you say, you did me a big favour. All of the evidence we had pointed to Arlene Jensen. It was her car and the eyewitness' description fitted her exactly. Jack Calloway ended up in some out of state sanitorium. The other guy, Arnold Henders, was badly busted up, both legs broken, smashed ribs and some other internal injuries. Last I heard he was living just outside of L.A.

'Jensen paid all of their expenses and gave them both a big handout. Guess that's why they never brought any charges — that, and the fact that someone leaned on them a bit.'

'Someone from the Mob?'

'What do you think?'

'I think you're right. Probably the same person who stopped the investigation and got you discharged when you tried to keep it going. But you've no idea who it was?'

'Ideas, yes. Proof — no.'

'Names?'

His eyes studied me and there was something in his expression I couldn't analyze. 'Manzelli,' he said finally.

'Thanks Joe.' I said, getting to my feet. 'I didn't hear that.'

I went to the bar, ordered two more whiskies and took them back to his table. He was still staring straight in front of him as if I was still sitting in the chair opposite.

I left him to return to his drunken memories and went out. The night air tasted good after the atmosphere inside The Oyster.

I knew I had to sleep on what I'd learned before I could make anything of it. There were too many big fish swimming around in the water — and one of them was a shark with big teeth. The problem was figuring out who it was.

The next morning very little of it still made any sense. But the fact that Manzelli might have been the one to shut down the police investigation into those two hit-and-run incidents troubled me. I'd had dealing with Manzelli before. They'd been fairly cordial that time but he was the Big Man who ran all of the gangs in L.A. Nothing happened without him knowing about it and he had the muscle to say what City Hall and the police did and when they did it. When he snapped his fingers, everyone jumped.

Naturally, he'd want to protect his own interests and if Arlene Jensen had got hold of something that could make trouble for him, he wouldn't hesitate to make sure it never became known.

My head was aching as if I'd spent the whole night on the town. I swallowed a couple of painkillers with my coffee but they didn't help much. I guess I was looking like the wreck of the Hesperus by the time I rode the elevator up to the office. There I found a little guy waiting outside the door.

'Johnny Merak?' he asked politely.

'That's right.' I unlocked the door and let him go in ahead of me. 'What can I do for you?'

At that moment, I was hoping he wasn't another potential client, probably looking for a missing wife. I had enough on my hands with the two I'd already got.

He stood just inside the door, looking around him, like a kid on his first day at school, not sure of anything.

'Take a seat,' I said. I hung my hat on the peg just inside the door, opened the window, then walked around him as he sat down.

'I'd no idea what your office hours were,' he said, almost apologetically.

'Sometimes I've no idea what they are myself.' I sat down facing him.

'As bad as that, eh?' He took out a pack of cigarettes, lit one and placed the spent match carefully in the ashtray. A guy with neat habits, I thought. 'My name's Carradine. Jed Carradine. Like you I'm a private investigator. I work for Barbara Winton.'

I nodded. 'She told me she'd hired someone to keep an eye on Charles Jensen. I suppose you know she's asked me to look into the disappearance of her sister.'

He sat back, blowing smoke into the air. He was somewhere in his mid-forties with close-cropped brown hair. His suit had seen better days but that was probably his working attire.

'She did mention that,' he acknowledged. 'I've no problem with it. But that isn't why I wanted to see you.'

'Go on,' I said as he paused uncertainly.

'I was hoping we might exchange information. All strictly confidential, of course. Not that I'm trying to interfere in anything you're handling and I know a lot of it won't go any further than this office.'

'Suits me,' I said. 'Just what do you have in mind?'

Carradine looked around the office with an idle, but searching, gaze, taking in everything. 'Do you get many big clients like Jensen and Miss Winton?'

'Not many,' I admitted. 'It's usually run of the mill stuff. Sometimes I get a big case like the Galecci murder a few months back.'

'I heard about that.' The cigarette smoke was now like a blanket around his face. 'But to get down to cases. As you probably know from my employer, I'm watching Jensen. She seems to think he's behind her sister's disappearance, possibly her murder. What's his connection with you?'

I shrugged. 'He simply wants me to follow his wife. Reckons she's seeing another man.'

'Another divorce?'

'I guess so. All he wants is concrete evidence so he doesn't have to pay out any alimony this time.'

'Have you got any?'

'Nothing so far. Jensen's not been in touch yet. Maybe there is some evidence to be got, maybe not.'

Carradine digested that for a minute, then he stubbed out his cigarette. The smoke thinned a little. 'All right,' he said finally. 'I'll give you something of what I've got. Most of the time Jensen spends on a big project he's got on the east side of L.A. Everything above board and perfectly legit. But every other Friday, he goes to a certain address on Bay Avenue, always late at night when there aren't too many nosy people around.'

'Except for yourself.'

He gave a faint smile at that. 'You've heard of Mike Corgan?'

'The racketeer? Sure; but what had he got to do with Jensen?'

'Everything, it seems. Like I said, Jensen goes to his place every fortnight and I don't think it's to play a friendly game of poker.'

He leaned forward and tapped on the desk with his fingers. 'My guess is Jensen's somehow tied in with the Mobs.'

'I'd already figured that,' I told him. 'You could've got that information from your client. But I reckon you wanted to check it out for yourself.'

He looked a trifle downhearted at that. I felt sorry for him. But you can't get every bit of information all at once. There's always some other guy who gets the important bits before you do.

'So are you still going through with his case?'

It was none of his business, but I said

quietly enough, 'Sure. I reckon his money is as good as the Devil's. At least it pays the rent.'

He made to say something more but at that moment, two things happened. Dawn opened the door and came in — and the phone on my desk buzzed like an impatient bee. It was the kind of buzz that suggested someone on the other end of the line wanted to say something urgent and important.

'Merak,' I said.

It was Ricardo. 'I've got some information I think you'd like to have,' he said. His voice sounded funny, as if he was breathing hard, but I guessed it was a bad line.

'Where can I meet you?' I asked.

'Same place. Half an hour.'

'I'll be there,' I said. There was a click as the line went dead.

Looking across at Carradine, I said, 'Sorry about that. One of my connections.'

'I understand.' He got up and walked to the door, pausing with his fingers around the knob. 'If I hear anything more, I'll be in touch.' The door closed behind him.

In answer to the look of mute inquiry on Dawn's face, I said, 'Jed Carradine, another private investigator. He works for Arlene's sister, trailing Charles Jensen.'

'Things are getting more and more complicated all the time,' she said. 'Aren't there such things as simple cases any more?'

'If there are, this certainly isn't one of them.'

She went over to the rear of the office. 'Have you had anything to drink this morning? Coffee?'

I shook my head. 'Much as I'd like another to clear my head, I have to meet someone just out of town. It sounded important.'

'One of these days you're going to drive yourself so deep into the ground they'll need a shovel to get you out,' she retorted.

I grinned and jammed on my hat. 'While I'm away, there's something more you can do for me. See if you can get any information on those two lawyers who were run down four years ago. Their names are Jack Calloway and Arnold Henders. Above all, try to find out where they are now.'

She wrote the names down on a small pad. 'You think either of them will talk?'

'Somehow, I doubt it. But if word gets around that I'm trying to contact them, whoever tried to make mincemeat out of them may be forced to show their hand. It's the only way I know of pushing this would-be killer into the open.'

Dawn's lips twisted into a tight line. 'With yourself as the target, I suppose?'

'That had crossed my mind,' I said. I left and made my way down into the street.

It was a little easier driving up into the hills in broad daylight even though the clear air and bright sunlight made everything look even more dilapidated and dismal when I finally turned off onto the rutted track. Maybe this area had looked great forty or so years back, boasting a panoramic view over the bay. Now it looked so empty and deserted I doubted if the rats still had a home there.

I spotted the car at the top of the slope and stopped the Merc halfway up. There was no sign of Ricardo. But then he wasn't a guy who liked wide open spaces where he could be spotted for miles if anyone was tailing him. He preferred to hide himself in crowds, just one anonymous face in hundreds of others.

Ricardo had driven the car off the track so that it was almost out of sight from below, behind a thick screen of bushes. I walked towards it, slowly, one step at a time, because there was something here that didn't quite add up. For almost two minutes, I wasn't sure what it was.

Then it hit me, right out of the blue.

The car engine was still running!

It wasn't like Ricardo not to cut the engine once he got to where he wanted to go. I pushed my way through the bushes with the acrid smell of dust and sage in my nostrils. There was a wide hollow and the car was parked in the middle of it. All of the windows were tight shut even though the temperature was somewhere approaching ninety in the shade.

I could just make out the figure seated

behind the wheel through the dusty glass but it wasn't that which caught, and held, my attention. It was the pipe leading from the exhaust, over the top, and through a narrow gap in the sunroof.

There didn't seem to be anyone around. At least, I couldn't see or hear anyone. Running forward, I grabbed the door handle and pulled. It opened on hinges that squeaked a little. The smell of the fumes hit me in a solid wave.

Reaching in front of Ricardo, I switched off the engine, then took out my handkerchief and placed it over my mouth and nose. Running around to the other side, I managed to open that door, then turned my attention to Ricardo. He was slumped forward, his face resting on the wheel. His hat was tilted awkwardly on his head.

Easing him back, I felt for the pulse, but there was nothing. His face was almost as blue as the ocean, his eyes wide and staring. By now, the fumes were beginning to clear. I put my handkerchief away and it was then I noticed two things that, to my naturally suspicious mind, told me he hadn't committed suicide.

There was a lump on the back of his head the size of an egg that had been hidden by his hat. And his shoes were covered in white dust.

Stepping back, I noticed the marks in the dusty ground just at the side of the door.

Someone had hit him on the back of the skull, just hard enough to knock him out, and then dragged him into the car, sitting him behind the wheel before setting everything up to make it look like he'd just got tired of life.

Whatever new information he'd had for me, he wasn't going to tell me now.

That was when a new thought struck me. Maybe there hadn't been any information; maybe that funny quality I'd noticed about his voice on the phone had been because there had been a gun in his back when he'd been speaking to me.

I turned to go back to the Merc, to drive back into town and report what I'd found to the cops. But quite suddenly there was a faint sound at my back, a barely audible swish in the air, and the sunlight went out as if there'd been an instantaneous eclipse.

When I opened my eyes again, the sunlight was back. It was streaming painfully into my eyes and I felt sick in my stomach. Those little mice had no chance to run around now. My head was stuffed full of cotton wool.

I forced my eyes to stay open, even though I could make out nothing but glaring brightness and a couple of blurred shadows directly in front of my vision.

I was lying on my back with pain lancing through my skull every time I tried to move, so I knew that whoever was there was standing over me, peering down into my face.

Swallowing hard, I rolled over onto my side and tried to get one hand under me to lever myself up. It didn't work.

'I reckon he's coming round now, Lieutenant.' The voice was one I knew I ought to recognize but it echoed in my ears as it there was a drum tattoo going on in the background.

Somehow, my vision focussed. Some of the blurriness faded and I could make out details a little more clearly. What I saw, however, was something I didn't like.

This wasn't the place where I'd found Ricardo's body. There was a steep drop-off to my right. A few straggling bushes that seemed to be growing there just because there was no better place nearby.

And right beside me, so close I could have reached out and touched her, a woman lay on her side facing me. But this was no lover's tryst.

There was an ugly red-purple hole in the middle of her forehead, just above the finely arched brows. Her lips were drawn back across perfect white teeth and her black hair shone bluely in the glaring sunlight.

I recognized the face at once. Dawn had shown it to me in the office.

Arlene Jensen! And this time there was absolutely no doubt about it.

She was very dead!

I somehow got to my knees, hung there for a full minute and then staggered upright. I put out my hand to hang onto something but there was nothing there.

Then someone gripped me by the upper arm. I turned slowly. Two men stood there. One I recognized as Sergeant Kolowinski. The other guy was shorter with a hard face that could have been carved on Mount Rushmore. I knew him but only by reputation. Lieutenant Shaun O'Leary.

He'd been promoted to take Lieutenant Donovan's place after I'd pinned Carlos Galecci's murder on Donovan. But I figured he wasn't going to do me any favours because of that. Word had it, however, that he was a straight cop who always did everything according to the book.

O'Leary walked over and went down on one knee beside Arlene while Kolowinski kept a tight hold on my arm.

'This isn't what it looks like,' I said. My mouth was dry but somehow I got the words out in a low mumble.

'Sure. But I reckon you've got a hell of a lot of explaining to do. My guess is that you're up to your neck in quicksand and sinking deeper every minute.'

O'Leary came back. His face hadn't

changed. If anything, it had hardened even further. He spoke to Kolowinski. 'Looks as though she's only been dead for around half an hour. Not much longer. Shot with a .38 but we won't know that for sure until we find the slug.'

He swung his attention to me. 'Okay, suppose you tell me who you are and what you're doing here?'

'The name's Merak,' I told him. 'I'm a private investigator. You can ask the sergeant here, he'll verify it.'

Kolowinski nodded. 'That's right, Lieutenant. I've known Johnny Merak for years.'

O'Leary frowned. 'The guy who put Donovan away?'

'That's right, Lieutenant,' I said. 'I hope you're not going to hold that against me.'

'Don't try to be funny with me, Merak. I've got enough evidence here to hold you for first-degree murder. Let me see your gun.'

I dug inside my jacket with my free hand. The holster was empty.

O'Leary smiled, but it wasn't a nice

smile. 'Mislaid your gun, Merak?'

'Not mislaid,' I said. 'Stolen would be a better word.'

'Of course.' He didn't believe me. I couldn't blame him in the circumstances. Whoever had done this had framed me tighter than the Mona Lisa. I didn't doubt that when they found the slug that had killed Arlene, it would match up with my gun and somewhere close by my .38 would be lying around with my prints all over it.

'Read him his rights, Sergeant and then take him down to the station. I'll question him later. In the meantime, I want a team up here to take this whole area apart. I'm pretty sure what we're going to find.'

Kolowinski went through the usual ritual and then pointed me in the direction of the track.

'What about my car?' I asked.

'Once I've checked it out, I'll drive it down to the station,' O'Leary said coldly. 'I don't think you'll be needing it for a while — if ever.'

There was no point in arguing. I got inside the patrol car beside Kolowinski. I noticed he didn't put the cuffs on me, probably for old time's sake. It was a nice gesture.

It was an even nicer one when he decided not to put me into one of the cells but left me sitting against the wall in front of the desk. I guess he figured I wasn't going to make a run for it.

O'Leary came in a couple of hours and six cigarettes later. He went through into his office at the back without looking in my direction. I waited for another fifteen minutes before he came back and motioned me to follow him.

Inside the office, he shut the door. Motioning me to the chair in front of the desk, he sat down opposite.

'All right, Merak. Let me hear your side of the story.'

'Do you mind if I smoke?' I asked.

There was no ashtray on the desk, but he opened a drawer and took one out, placing it in front of me.

I lit up, blew the smoke through my nostrils, then told him as fully as I could remember the events leading up to my regaining consciousness beside Arlene

Jensen. He didn't interrupt once, sitting there with his hard eyes on me, his fingertips pressed together in a fleshy pyramid.

Then he said coldly, 'Now let me tell you how I see it. You arranged to meet this petty hoodlum Ricardo to get some information out of him. Knowing his kind, I'd say he wouldn't spill anything important unless you paid him. When you didn't, he clammed up and threatened you with the Mob. That's when you decided to kill him and make it look like suicide.

'Only for some reason, Arlene Jensen turned up and she had to be silenced as well. That fits the facts — as far as I know them.'

'It's a swell theory,' I said. 'Only I didn't kill Ricardo. He'd already given me plenty only last night. There was no reason for him to double-cross me.'

'So you say someone else killed Ricardo, then knocked you cold, took your gun and shot Arlene Jensen?'

'It's an even better theory than yours.' I pointed out. 'Unless you figure I killed

Ricardo, shot Arlene who just happened to be taking a stroll in that god-forsaken spot, hid my gun somewhere, and then somehow coshed myself on the back of the head and went to sleep beside her body. If I'd done that, you'd have found the blackjack next to me. But you didn't, did you?'

There was an icy grimace on his face now. But it somehow seemed artificial.

'All right,' he agreed finally. 'We didn't find any blackjack, or anything like it, in the area. But maybe you can enlighten me on one puzzling thing.'

'What's that, Lieutenant?'

'What was Arlene Jensen doing up there? I don't believe for one minute she went there with Ricardo. But there was no sign of another car, not even tracks. And Ricardo wasn't the type she usually associated with. But I do know you've been hired to find her.'

'Oh, who told you that?'

O'Leary gave a frosty smile. 'Miss Winton, her sister. Seems she was damned sure her sister had been murdered four years ago. Since then she hadn't been seen. Now she turns up really dead and no one seems to know where she's been all this time.'

He leaned forward and stared hard at me across the desk. 'We also know that you reported some woman driving a dark blue Chrysler tried to kill you a couple of nights back.'

'So you figured that might provide a motive for me wanting to make sure she didn't try it again?' I tried to keep the sarcasm out of my voice. O'Leary might be a straight cop but he had a fiery temper that went with his Irish ancestry.

'In this game, anything's possible. I've got men searching that area right now. What are the odds they'll come up with your gun and only your prints on it?'

'I'd say it's highly likely. Whoever planned this wouldn't miss out on a chance like that to plant the incriminating evidence on me.'

'This may surprise you, Merak. That's the way I see it too.'

'Huh?' I was surprised. Nothing had changed in O'Leary's expression.

'Your story gets more fantastic as it

goes on. I may be wrong, but I figure you're telling the truth. Your secretary confirms that phone call you got. I can't understand why you'd want to kill one of your contacts even if he was on the wrong side of the law. But if you're holding anything back from me and maybe thinking you can make yourself a little publicity out of this case, forget it right now. This is a police matter and I want you to stay out of my hair. Got that?'

'Sure thing, Lieutenant,' I said.

'All right. You can go now. But don't take any unexpected trips out of town. I may want to talk to you again.'

I got up. Halfway to the door, I turned and said, 'Just a couple of things, Lieutenant. Do I get my gun back when you've finished checking it over?'

'I'll think about that,' he said dryly.

'And how come you and the sergeant just happened to be up there around the time all this happened?'

He hesitated at that and I thought he wasn't going to reply. Then he said coolly, 'We got an anonymous tip-off that there'd been shots fired up there.'

I went out.

My head was still pounding like the Pacific surf and it hurt whenever I moved my neck. But the cotton wool inside my skull had gone and I was beginning to think more rationally.

Somehow, I made it back to the office. Dawn wasn't there and I figured she was still out trying to get the lowdown on those two lawyers.

I felt the back of my head as I stood at the window looking out at the traffic. It felt as though a hole had been bashed into my skull. The noise from the traffic came through the open window like rollers on the ocean. I still felt woozy from that crack on the head but I'd get over it.

Dawn arrived fifteen minutes later, took one look at me and said,

'God, Johnny! You look a mess. What happened?'

'It was a set-up, a real peach. I should have figured there was something funny about that phone call.'

'You mean it wasn't the man you were supposed to meet?'

'Oh, it was the right guy. But by the time I got there, he was dead.'

She put the notes she'd made on the desk and then plugged in the electric kettle and switched it on. Over her shoulder, she said, 'I got a call from the police department while I was at the newspaper offices. Don't ask me how they knew I was there. They asked about that phone call. I wasn't sure what was happening.'

While she made the coffee, black and strong, I told her about Ricardo and Arlene Jensen. The coffee was ready when I finished and I poured a slug of the office whisky into it despite Dawn's look of disapproval.

'So it figures that whoever gave that anonymous tip-off to the police was the one who killed them both.'

'That's a fairly safe bet,' I said. 'And fortunately for me, O'Leary goes along with it. Even if the caller didn't do the actual killing, he knew what was to happen and for some reason, I'd been picked as the patsy to take the rap.'

Dawn smiled down at me, then bent to

examine the bump on the back of my head. 'Then I think someone is going to be very sore and disappointed when they hear the police have let you go.'

'Maybe that's one of the reasons O'Leary didn't charge me with murder,' I said thoughtfully. 'It's more than likely that whoever it was will have another try. What I can't figure out is — why me?'

'Could it be that someone who's hired you is now regretting it because there's a chance you'll dig up something they want to keep hidden?'

I sipped the coffee. It tasted good. 'You think it's Jensen?'

'Why not? I'd say he's always wanted Arlene out of the way and somehow, he found out where she's been hiding. He could also have known about your visit to Barbara Winton and guessed you may have uncovered his links with the Mob.'

'Sometimes, you think as smart as I'm supposed to be,' I said.

'And sometimes you're not as smart as you think you are, nearly getting yourself killed and then arrested for first-degree murder.'

'Touché.' I finished my coffee even though it burned my throat and set the cup down on the desk. 'Did you find out anything about those two lawyers?'

She went over and picked up her notes, then sat on the edge of the desk. Her leg brushed against mine. 'There's not much. It's old news and I'm sure a lot was given only in the police records of the time and they seem to have vanished.'

'Any idea where those two guys are now?'

'Calloway suffered brain damage in the accident. He's in a private sanitorium someplace but apparently he doesn't even know what year it is.'

'And Henders?'

'That's a little more hopeful. Seems he lives with his mother. I've got his last known address. A house in Bay City. He suffered broken bones and a lot of internal injuries. He can't walk but it seems his mind is all right.'

'Then if he reckons it was Arlene who tried to kill him and he learns she's now dead, he might open up and talk to me.'

5

Half an hour later I got a phone call from the precinct. My car was no longer a part of their murder inquiry and was being returned to me. There was no apology but then I hadn't expected one. I saw it appear in the street below the office fifteen minutes later.

Sergeant Kolowinski got out. He looked up and I gave him a wave from the window. He didn't wave back.

They hadn't given me my gun back and I felt as naked as a newborn babe without it.

I went back to the desk and picked up the piece of paper where Dawn had written the address for Arnold Henders. I figured there was no time like the present to pay him a visit. It was a beautiful sunny afternoon, just the day for a drive out.

The address was a large, rambling house with spacious grounds to the front and narrower lawns at the sides. Several tall palm trees grew near one wall and in the shade of one of them a man sat in a wheelchair.

I drove past the house and parked a little way along the street, then walked back. The iron gates were wide with metal figurings along the top and there was a red gravel drive, just as wide, leading up to the front of the house. This was clearly the affluent part of Bay City where the folks had real dough.

As I pushed open one of the gates, I wondered where Henders had got the mine of money to keep a place like this. His law career had been nipped in the bud by that accident and unless Jensen was still paying him, I guessed it had to be his mother who had the money.

There was a black Packard parked near the front door. It looked as though it could do with a good clean but it was the kind of car you use when you want to get from one side of the country to the other in a hurry.

My shoes made no sound as I turned off the drive onto the grass and walked towards the palm trees. It was like walking on that lush carpet in Barbara Winton's room at the *Drayton*.

The man in the wheelchair looked up sharply as I approached. He was tall, well-built, around thirty-five. I guessed he'd probably been a top ball player for some university in his younger days.

'Mister Henders?' I said.

'That's right.' There was a table beside him with a bottle and glass on it. The glass was half full of an amber liquid. In spite of his physical condition, he certainly wasn't going to do without the luxuries of life.

'My name's Merak. I'm a private investigator,' I told him, handing him my card. 'If you've no objection, I'd like to ask you a few questions.'

'What kind of questions?' He was instantly on the defensive.

'About your accident. I understand it happened four years ago. There was apparently an eyewitness who described the car that hit you and also the driver. A woman with jet-black hair.'

'I'm afraid I know nothing about that,' he replied stiffly. 'I spent several months in hospital and, as you can see, this is how I ended up.'

'I'm sorry,' I said. 'Both about your accident and having to intrude on you like this but it is important I get at the facts in this case.'

He eased himself into a more comfortable position, grimacing as if the effort still hurt him. 'Really, there's absolutely nothing I can tell you that I haven't already told the police. It was a long time ago and I'm trying to forget it and get on with my life, such as it is.'

I felt like a cigarette but there was no ashtray on the small table and, somehow, it seemed like sacrilege to flick ash onto the perfect lawn.

'May I tell you what I think, Mister Henders? You can contradict me if you like. I think you know the identity of the woman who tried to kill you. I think it was Arlene Jensen.'

His face took on a frightened look at that. I could see it in his eyes. If he could have walked, I'm sure he would have got up and run for the house, going inside, and locking the door on me.

Before he could utter a vehement denial, I went on, 'If I'm right, you've no cause to think she may try it again. She's not going to do anything again.'

'What do you mean?'

'Arlene Jensen is dead. They found her body up in the hills yonder. She'd been shot through the head.'

For a moment, I thought a miracle was about to happen and he'd leap out of the chair. His right hand reached out and grabbed my wrist. 'How do you know that? I've heard nothing about it.'

'I just happened to be there at the time. Whoever shot her also killed a petty crook named Ricardo.'

He let go of my wrist, picked up the glass from the table, and downed the amber contents in a single swallow. Evidently that made him feel better. Some of the colour came back into his face.

'You're sure it was Arlene Jensen? Absolutely sure. There's no mistake?'

'No doubt about it,' I told him. 'Someone coshed me on the back of the head and when I woke up I was lying on the ground right next to her.'

He said nothing. He didn't even move.

'Was it Arlene who tried to kill you?' I asked.

He licked his lips. Then he moved his arm and poured himself another drink. His hand was shaking slightly.

Then he said, 'I'll be perfectly honest with you. I've always believed it was her. I never saw the driver's face clearly. Everything happened so fast. I was just crossing the street when this car jumped a red light and came straight at me. All I really saw was this long, jet-black hair. The next thing I knew, I woke up in a hospital bed.'

'You're aware that your colleague received the same treatment as you within a few days. Only he wasn't quite so lucky.'

'The police told me about him. That's what made me so sure it was Arlene Jensen. The only thing I had in common with Jack Calloway was that we both represented her husband in the divorce case. Nothing else.'

'There were also some threatening letters you received.'

'Sure. But I thought nothing of them at the time. We sometimes got such hate mail, particularly from clients who thought things went wrong for them because of our fault.'

'Nevertheless, I find it hard to believe anyone would try to kill the lawyers, no matter how angry they were about things. It seems far more likely they'd make a try for the ex-husbands.'

'Who knows what people like Arlene are capable of if they're mad enough?'

I looked at him hard. 'How do you mean? Mad as in angry, or mad as in insane?'

He made an impatient gesture with his left hand. 'I'm not insinuating that she was insane by any stretch of the imagination. But she was as sore as hell about some of the evidence we had to present to the judge regarding her adultery.'

'Did you know Arlene personally? I mean, were you ever on speaking terms?'

Before he could reply, there was the sound of a door slamming loudly somewhere at my back. I turned my head sharply to the right. The woman who came striding purposefully across the lawn in our direction looked appreciably older than Arnold and I figured she had to be his mother. She had a square, weather-beaten face and she wore no make-up. Her body was broad. She could have passed for a bouncer at any of the nightclubs in L.A.

'May I ask who you are, young man?' she demanded roughly. Her tone had a brittle edge to it that warned me I'd better have a damned good reason for being there, otherwise there would be trouble. 'And what are you doing on my property? If you've come to annoy my son, you can leave right this minute. He's not talking to any more nosy reporters.'

'I'm not a reporter, Mrs. Henders.' I gave her my biggest, warmest smile. She looked quite capable of grabbing me by the collar and hauling me off the property without any effort. 'I simply wanted to ask him a few questions concerning his accident.'

'If you're not a reporter, who are you? A cop?'

'Not a cop,' I assured her. I knew I had to pick my words with care.

'I'm a private investigator.'

'So you think that allows you to come here without permission, snoop around, try to rake up the past. My son's had enough trouble these past four years. I'm doing my damnedest to let him get on with his life and forget all that.'

'I'm sure you are,' I said.

At that, Henders spoke up. 'Arlene Jensen is dead, mother. That's what Mister Merak came to tell me.'

Something like a nasty light lit up briefly in the woman's hard, blue eyes. Then she muttered, 'So she's finally dead. Good riddance, I say. That's all that murdering bitch deserved. I'm glad to hear it.'

Evidently, Mrs. Henders shared the same low opinion of Arlene Jensen as her son did.

'I suppose there are some people who get to you like that,' I remarked.

Her lips clamped down so tightly they almost disappeared above the double chin. She wasn't sure whether I was being deliberately sarcastic or agreeing with her. Then she said thickly, 'Well — if that's all you came here for, I think you'd better leave.'

She threw Arnold a funny look that I couldn't analyze.

I pulled the brim of my hat down a little and moved away. Mrs. Henders fell into step beside me like a bulldog on a leash, making sure I didn't stray on the way out.

As we stepped onto the gravel drive, I said, 'That's a nice car you've got there. I suppose you have to do all the driving around now that your son isn't able to.'

'I don't drive,' she snapped harshly. 'Lazy habit. That car has been parked there for four years now. It was Arnold's. I've threatened to get rid of it several times but he insists it's the only link he has between now and the days when he was going right to the top of his profession.'

She twisted her head on the thick neck to glare directly at me. Maybe she thought I was going to make some facetious remark.

'You think that's stupid of him?'

'Not in the least,' I said hastily, keeping a straight face. 'Seeing him like that, I reckon one can get pretty frustrated and angry at the way life's treated you. If it gives him something solid to hang onto — why not?'

She saw me to the gate. I didn't turn my head as I walked back to where I'd parked the Merc but I could feel those hard, blue eyes drilling into the back of my neck all the way. She was still there, standing like the Grim Reaper when I turned the car, then parked it on the opposite side of the road facing towards town.

I sat there and waited until she got tired of watching and went back to the house. There was something about that set-up which jarred on my mind. I couldn't figure out exactly what it was. Maybe, I told myself, she was just being the over-protective mother, desperately keeping her son out of touch with the nasty outside world.

On the other hand, maybe they had something to hide. I'd seen that funny

106

look she'd given Arnold; a warning kind of look, as if he'd been on the point of saying something she didn't want me to know. I sighed. Perhaps that was just my nasty suspicious mind coming to the fore again.

I drove back into town. Dawn was still in the office and I also had a visitor — Lieutenant O'Leary.

He was sitting in the chair in front of my desk. He didn't get up as I went in. I noticed that my gun was lying on top of the desk in front of him.

As I sat down, he took some papers from his inside pocket and pushed them across to me.

'I've decided to let you have your gun back, Merak,' he said. 'Against my better judgment. Sign both copies of these.'

I took out my pen and signed them. He took one back. 'As we figured, there were only your prints on that gun and it was possibly the one used to kill Arlene Jensen. One shot had been fired and whoever took it didn't make much of an attempt to hide it.'

He leaned back. 'However, we found

no trace of the slug.'

'That doesn't surprise me,' I said.

His brows went up until they met in a straight line. 'Now why do you say that?' he asked.

'Because the way I figure it, Arlene wasn't killed there. She was shot someplace else and her body taken there, almost certainly in the boot of a car.'

'Ricardo's?'

I shrugged. 'That's as good a guess as any right now. There's one thing I am damned sure of. When Ricardo phoned me asking me to meet him there, he had a gun in his back. It was a put-up job to pin Arlene's murder on me. Unfortunately for Ricardo, he'd know the identity of the killer so he had to go too.'

O'Leary's face didn't change but I knew he was turning the possibility over in his mind, trying to find a hole in it. Then he shook his head.

'A good theory, Merak. There's just one thing about it that doesn't tally. The boys at the precinct went over Ricardo's car with a toothcomb. There wasn't a trace of blood in the boot — or anywhere else.'

I lit a cigarette and blew the smoke towards the ceiling. 'Then we're left with two possibilities. Either the killer is a very careful guy who takes everything into consideration, and he wrapped the body completely before putting it into the car, or — '

'Or there were two cars involved,' Dawn put in.

O'Leary rubbed a hand across his chin. It made a scratching noise like a stuck gramophone needle. 'In that case, the killer had an accomplice because if he was as careful as you figure, he wouldn't allow Ricardo to drive his own car. There would always be the chance that punk would give him the slip somewhere along the way.'

'That could fit the facts as far as we know them, if it was a Mob slaying. Ricardo was a punk like you say. He was in with the Mob. That's why he'd never meet me in any of the dives in L.A. It had always to be some out-of-the-way place with nobody around.'

I could see that O'Leary didn't like that idea. He was a straight cop and he'd do his duty according to the book, but tangling with the mobs could get real messy and he wouldn't want to go down that road unless he had real evidence.

'Then why Arlene Jensen? So far as we know, she had no ties with anything illegal.'

His eyes grew icy. 'Unless you know something about her that I don't. If you do, you'd better spill it.' He made a sharp movement with his hand against the desk as if swatting an invisible fly that was irritating him. Quite suddenly, he was suspicious.

'I don't have any evidence against her at all,' I said smoothly. 'Besides, there's such a thing as client confidentiality and — '

'I don't give a damn about client confidentiality!' He almost shouted the words. His face was turning a pale shade of crimson. 'Don't hold out on me Merak. I can always take the gun back.'

I looked up at the ceiling, then back to O'Leary. I knew he meant every word he said. Shrugging, I said, 'Okay, Lieutenant, I'll tell you what I've heard. But I want you to know all of this is just hearsay. I've no real facts as yet to back it up.'

'Go on.' He spoke through his teeth. 'Let's have it.'

'Charles Jensen is a client of mine. He's hired me to follow his wife — thinks she may be seeing some other guy behind his back. I've spoken to two of my contacts. Ricardo was one. The other is an ex-cop who worked on the hit-and-run cases and got pushed off the force when he disagreed with the order from the top to close the files. Both of them say that Jensen is working hand in glove with some very shady characters where his construction business is concerned. Whether it's getting lucrative contracts or something else, I don't know.

'But apparently Arlene found this out and it's possible she was about to blackmail him once he got the divorce. If those hoods who're backing Jensen to the hilt discovered this, they'd want to silence her permanently.'

O'Leary nodded slightly. 'Did you see any other car up there?'

'No. Only Ricardo's where he'd driven

it into that canyon out of sight.'

He nodded. 'And I'm damned sure no one passed us on that road when we turned off the highway to go up there.'

'So, if we're right, there has to be another way down,' I said.

His eyes narrowed down to mere slits. Then his face cleared. It was like the dawn breaking over a barren landscape. 'I don't know that area particularly well but there is a rough track, nothing more than that, leading down from the hills and coming out somewhere near the main coast highway north of Bay City. It would be a rough ride, but I guess it's possible. Whoever did this would know we were on our way there so it would be the only way they could get away without being seen.'

'Couldn't they have parked somewhere well away from the scene, waited there until you'd gone, then head back into town along the mountain road?' Dawn asked.

O'Leary shook his head. 'I don't think so. They'd have no idea how big an area we'd search. There were five of my men up there looking for that gun and the slug that killed Arlene. It would be too big a risk for them to take.'

He jammed his hat down tighter on his head and got up. 'I'll bear all of this in mind, Merak. Thanks for this latest piece of information. If you learn anything more, particularly where it concerns Jensen, you let me know at once.'

'Sure,' I said. 'In the meantime I'll go along with him and keep an eye on his present wife. I wouldn't like the same thing to happen to her.'

'Neither would I,' he said as he left.

The way he said it made me feel like her guardian angel.

6

I was standing by the side of my bed, staring out of the window at nothing. Even if I'd been staring at anything, there was nothing in the view of any interest. The same old street with the same early morning traffic moving in long queues along it.

It was going to be another hot Friday with only the dust moving as if it had anywhere to go. I was still getting the occasional twinge in my head where I'd been coshed and was debating whether to take a couple of painkillers with my first coffee of the day when the phone on the bedside table rang.

The sound jarred through my aching skull like a drop-hammer. I couldn't figure out who would be calling me on that line. Clients usually called my office. I picked up the receiver and held it gently to my right ear.

'Is that you, Merak?' said the voice. It

was Charles Jensen's dulcet tones.

Somehow, I snapped myself alert.

'Yes, Mister Jensen.'

'I'm calling you on your own phone rather than your office number,' he said. 'It's much safer this way and I wanted to get you before you left. Janine has just announced she's going to see her sister this evening. She says she'll be away for a couple of days.'

'So you want me to tail her?'

'Of course. I'm hoping you'll get me some results. You know where I live. I want you to be there by seven this evening. She'll be driving the blue Chrysler.'

I jerked as if someone had hit me in the face. A blue Chrysler! Coincidence?

Somehow, I didn't think so. Sure there were plenty of blue Chryslers cruising the streets of L.A. And maybe I was reading more into this than there really was. The description I'd been given of the dame who'd warned me off the case certainly didn't fit Janine.

'You still there, Merak?'

'What — ? Sure, I'm here,' I said.

'You know exactly what you have to do. Whatever happens, don't lose her. She's been acting oddly of late. She may be suspicious and try to throw you off the trail if she suspects anyone might be following her.'

'I'll be careful. This isn't the first case like this I've worked on.'

'No, I'm sure it isn't. But there's too much at stake here for any slip-up and — '

The phone went dead before he finished what he meant to say. I guessed that Janine had probably walked into the room unexpectedly and he had to cut the message short.

I went into the small kitchenette, put the kettle on to boil, spooned coffee into a cup and waited for the kettle to start steaming.

Then I made the coffee and went back into the bedroom to drink it.

There were so many things going through my mind. I felt as though I was on some out-of-control carousel, spinning like a top and unable to get off. Somewhere, there was an answer that made some kind of sense. At the moment, however, I couldn't find it.

Had it been Janine who had given that little runt a twenty note to pass on that warning? Looking at it objectively, in the cold light of day, it didn't seem so absurd as I'd first thought. A black wig, knowing the guy would give me this description — and she was certainly the logical one to know her husband had been to see me.

Sipping my coffee, I tried to follow that idea through to see if I could reach a logical conclusion. Knowing her husband had been to see me was one thing; knowing why was another. She may have figured Charles had guessed that she knew too much about his business partners and it was just possible that if I started poking my nose in, I could find out more about her than she wanted her husband to know, especially if she was considering the highly dangerous game of blackmail.

A lot would depend on whether I could find out who she really went to meet. If it was just another guy who provided her with something she lacked at home, I could be on the wrong track altogether.

I passed the day in the office trying to work things out. Dawn busied herself with the day-to-day matters. There were no further phone calls, not that I was expecting any. All in all, it was a very quiet, boring day.

The sultry heat reached its peak sometime in the early afternoon and didn't seem to lessen even when the sun started dipping in the direction of the ocean.

Dawn left at the usual time and I sat there in the silence watching the hands on my watch go round. By the time it got to six-thirty, I got up, locked the office, and rode the elevator down to the car park.

The traffic had thinned by now and I got down the highway without much trouble before turning off onto Melavar Drive. It was a wide curve of elegant, white-fronted buildings that looked as though they had come straight out of a Hollywood movie. All had high stone walls around them with big iron gates and trees planted in just the right places.

Once I came within sight of Jensen's

address, I slowed and then parked fifty yards away from the closed gates. My watch said five minutes before seven. Leaving the engine running, I settled back behind the wheel, my hat pulled down a little so that the brim shaded my eyes from the glare of the setting sun.

I wondered if Janine was one of those few women for whom punctuality meant something. I didn't have to wait too long to find out. At precisely seven, the big gates opened and the blue Chrysler appeared. Janine was at the wheel, her long blonde hair clearly visible through the car window.

She made a sharp turn onto the Drive. I waited until she was almost out of sight before pulling away from the kerb. She wasn't hurrying, but she wasn't dawdling either, just keeping to a steady fifty. I followed her onto the main coast highway, keeping well behind, occasionally allowing a couple of other cars to slip in between us. Pretty soon, it was clear she was heading out of town.

I settled down for a long drive. There was another two hours of daylight left. If she intended driving on through the dark, I'd have to close the distance between us to keep her in sight and that was when things might get a little tricky.

We were now driving into more open country. Occasionally, the ocean showed to my left. I had the window open and you could smell the tang in the air. Some big trucks were hauling north, a few showing their lights.

So far, Janine had given no indication she was aware anyone was on her tail. She stuck to the highway and stuck to the same steady speed as when she'd set out. One thing was for sure. If she stayed with the highway, she certainly wasn't heading for Cleveland where her sister was supposed to live. She was headed out into the country and unless she intended driving well into the night, I couldn't figure out where she was heading.

By the time it got dark and I was forced to switch on the headlights, I had edged up until I was less than fifty yards behind her exhaust. The traffic had now dwindled appreciably until there was scarcely any other car or truck on the road apart from ourselves.

There was an air of loneliness about the countryside now. Hills to my right, black shapes that looked like they had been painted on canvas and a sky above me where the stars had a more mellow glow about them than they did in winter.

I had an infrared camera and a pair of powerful binoculars on the passenger seat beside me. Jensen had provided the camera by messenger a couple of days earlier. I'd heard about these new gadgets but I'd never had the need for them before. I just hoped I'd get the chance to use it.

An hour passed and then, almost before I was aware of it, the tail lights of the Chrysler disappeared. I cut my speed, peering through the windscreen into the night. For a moment, I figured she'd got wise to me and had switched off her lights. Then I made out the side road twenty yards ahead to the right.

I swung the car around an acutely-angled turn, wrestling with the wheel as the tires skidded on the uneven road surface. The tail lights appeared again, just visible some distance ahead. By now, I reckoned that Janine must have noticed that whoever had been behind her on the highway was still sticking to her like glue.

She may have thought it was just someone who happened to be on the same road as herself, maybe heading for the same place. More likely, she might begin to think she had a tail on her.

A car, with its headlights full on, came blazing along the other side of the road.

The lights blinded me. For a moment, I could see nothing but a green haze that danced across the windscreen in front of me. I instinctively eased my foot off the accelerator as a white-painted fence appeared with an arrow pointing to the left.

The Merc scraped one of the posts. I had a vision of smashing through the fence, hitting nothing but air, and then dropping several hundred feet before hitting the ground. Miraculously, the car slewed back onto the road.

There was no sign of Janine. Swearing under my breath, I eased the Merc forward. For some time, the road had been climbing, twisting and turning like a chicane. Now, I suddenly realized I had almost reached the top. In front of me, the road was just visible where it formed a grey scar down the hillside.

Still no sign of any red tail lights.

But there was something else. Lights were visible on both sides of the road. A lot of lights. Some big roadhouse, I figured. Though why anyone would want to build one here, in the wilds, miles from anywhere. Unless those clients who used it had some reasons of their own for seeking seclusion.

But it figured. If Janine was meeting someone in secret, this was the ideal place for such a tryst.

I eased the Merc down the hill. The place was much bigger than I'd imagined, split in two; a huge building on one side of the road and about forty chalets on the other.

I turned into the spacious car park. More than two dozen cars were parked there in neat rows. Most of them were big, new models. Evidently, this place was no cheap dive or a pull-up joint for truckers. The people who came here, for whatever reason, had dough. Real dough. The perfect spot for an adulterous tryst.

I parked the Merc on the side furthest from the building and cut the engine. Somehow, it looked terribly shabby and out of place there.

Getting out, I soon located the Chrysler. Janine Jensen was nowhere to be seen.

Now I'd tracked Janine down, I had some decisions to make. This wasn't going to be as easy or straightforward as I'd imagined. There seemed to be no one around in the car park. Maybe whoever owned this joint reckoned that it was so isolated they didn't need any guards.

I had it figured for some kind of gambling joint, outside the city limits, which also provided accommodation for their guests. Whether or not it was run by the Mob, they'd certainly have a finger in it somewhere.

That meant that unless you were a member, you'd have no more chance of getting in than the Devil would getting past the pearly gates.

Since there was no one around, I decided to case the place first.

Then I had an idea that might get me in. It was risky, but there was a chance it might work. It was the only chance I had of checking on Janine and her mystery partner.

I checked the gun inside my coat and walked towards the side of the building. I was halfway towards it when the sound of voices brought me to a stop. I eased myself down between a couple of the cars. A small group of people had emerged from one of the chalets on the opposite side of the road and were making their way across it.

Two men and two women. All dressed to the nines. I waited until they'd gone inside. Then I walked quickly across the park until I was standing against the wall. There were too many lights streaming from the windows for my liking; too few shadows in which to hide —

For a couple of minutes I stood there in the silence and listened.

Then I inched my way to one side and risked a quick glance through the nearest window. There were large crystal chandeliers inside the room. A number of roulette tables and others where faro, poker and blackjack were being played.

I couldn't see Janine but then, I figured she hadn't come there to gamble. She was there for more serious business and it was my job to find out what it was.

Pulling my tie straight, I walked around to the front door. The big neon sign said 'Trocadero'. Just inside an array of lights winked on and off. Beyond them, two bouncers dressed discreetly in black suits stood on either side of the doors. They looked very efficient. One of them stepped forward, quiet as a shadow, as I went inside.

His companion stood quite still, looking at nothing, but watching everything.

The big guy looked me up and down. His face was as expressionless as a wooden Indian. 'Are you a member here, sir?' His voice seemed to come out of a gravel mixer.

'Not at the moment,' I said. 'But depending upon what this place has to offer, I might consider it.'

He showed his big teeth in a grin. It wasn't meant to be funny or pleasant.

'I'm afraid the membership is closed for the time being. I suggest you get back into your car and leave. I'm sure you'll find somewhere in L.A. more suited to your taste.'

'I'm sure I would,' I said. 'But you know how it is. Sometimes a change of venue provides a little more excitement.'

The second guy took a step forward. I could see they weren't sure whether I was a cop or belonged to one of the mobs. 'I don't think you'd like the kind of excitement we provide here,' he said gravely.

'Now that's strange.' I said. 'A friend of mine assured me I'd find everything I was looking for here. An important friend.'

The grin grew even broader, more menacing. 'How important?' he asked with a sideways glance at his companion.

'Pretty big in L.A.,' I replied. 'Sam Rizzio.'

The grin slipped. I knew from his expression that the name meant a lot to him. Rizzio had been Carlos Galecci's

second-in-command and the prime suspect for Galecci's murder before I'd got
him off the hook by nailing Lieutenant
Donovan. Whether that would be enough
for him to vouch for me, or even
remember me, was something I didn't
know.

'You're a friend of Rizzio's?'

'Let's say we've been quite close in the
recent past.'

The first guy seemed to make up his
mind. 'Follow me,' he said abruptly. I
followed him across the gambling room.
There was a door at the side where he
paused and knocked politely.

A voice said something from inside and
my guide pushed the door open and I
stepped through. The bouncer came
through after me, closing the door behind
him.

The man sitting behind the desk was
short with black hair slicked back. It
shone in the light. There were several gold
rings on his fingers. He had hawk-like
features with a thin, pinched nose and a
mouth that puckered up at the edges. His
eyes were like polished steel. They flashed

inquiringly in the bouncer's direction.

'This guy came in asking for membership, Mister Donero. I told him the membership is closed but he reckons he's a friend of Sam Rizzio.'

The pencil thin brows went up slightly. 'You're acquainted with Rizzio?' He looked straight at me as he spoke. His voice had a nasal hiss like a snake.

'You could say I saved his life a while back when he was suspected of killing Galecci,' I said.

He thought about that for a while. Then he said coldly. 'I presume you came here for a purpose and don't insult my intelligence by saying you merely wish to try your luck at the tables. You obviously don't have that kind of dough. I'd say you're either a cop or a nosy dick.'

'Does that make any difference?' I asked innocently.

His eyes glinted dangerously. 'If you're here to snoop around and annoy my guests, you're a very foolish man. We're very remote here. People can sometimes go missing in these hills.'

'I can believe it,' I said. 'It helps though

if they leave word about exactly where they're going.'

Donero began tapping the desk absently. Then he stopped. 'Just what is it you're after, Mister — ?'

'Merak,' I said. 'Private investigator.'

'Mister Merak.'

'Nothing to do with any case I'm working on.' I tried to speak casually. 'Even private investigators like a little flutter now and again. It breaks the monotony.'

He knew I was lying, but he said, 'You may find the stakes a little too high for you.'

'Perhaps,' I said. 'But don't you think you'd better check my credentials with Sam Rizzio?'

'I was just on the point of doing that,' he said thinly. He reached for the phone on his desk. He dialled a number. I guessed he'd had dealings with Rizzio before and knew the number off by heart.

There was a pause and then he spoke into the phone. Evidently he'd got straight through to Rizzio. I heard him give my name. He spoke a bit more and then he handed the phone to me. 'Rizzio wants a word with you,' he said shortly.

I took the receiver from him. 'Merak,' I said.

'What the hell are you up to, Merak?' He didn't sound too pleased. 'And how did you get to that place?'

'I just heard about it from a friend,' I lied. 'Believe me, Sam, I'm not here to make any trouble.'

There was a sound like a dry chuckle at the other end of the line.

'Take it from me, Merak, no one goes there to make any trouble. If they do, Donero makes damned sure they never leave.' There was a note of sardonic amusement in his voice. He knew I was there for something but he couldn't figure out what it was. However, I guessed he knew I wasn't so stupid as to make any trouble for the Mob.

After a long pause, he said, 'Put me back onto Donero.'

I handed the receiver back. Donero listened for a couple of minutes and then put it down. The eyes had changed. They still glinted like polished steel but there was a new light in them.

Finally, he said, 'I don't know how you got in with Rizzio but he okays you. Even suggests we should let you stay the night for free.'

'Now that's real nice of him,' I said. I was beginning to breathe a little easier but the sweat was still cold on the back of my neck and between my shoulders.

'However, as I've made clear, we don't want any trouble here and if you're interested in any of our guests, you keep that business until you leave tomorrow before noon. Is that understood?'

'Perfectly, Mister Donero,' I nodded. 'When I see Rizzio again, I'll thank him personally.'

He stared at me and his left hand began tapping the desk again. I knew he was trying to figure me out but the talk with Rizzio seemed to have taken his mind off getting rid of me; at least, for the time being.

His glance flicked to the bouncer standing mutely at my elbow. 'Show Mister Merak to a chalet.'

He was itching to have the bruiser take

me apart and force me to tell the truth as to why I was there. But however much it galled him, nobody disobeyed an order from Sam Rizzio. Now that he had control of the biggest of the mobs in L.A. he was second only to Manzeli.

I turned to go.

'Just one more thing, Merak. You'll leave that gun you're carrying with me. Just a precaution, of course.' His voice was silkily smooth.

'But I — ' I began.

'A rule of the house,' he said. His smile had a menacing quality about it. 'As you may realize, our clientele come from all walks of life and if we allowed them to walk around with guns, there's no telling what might happen. You'll get it back the minute you leave.'

There was nothing I could do. I took the .38 from its holster and placed it carefully on the desk in front of him. He picked it up, checked it, then opened the top drawer of his desk and put it inside.

The big guy held the door open for me as we went out, back through the gaming room and out into the fresh air.

We crossed the road together. A small group of people came out of one of the chalets. None of them was Janine Jensen. They gave me funny looks as they walked past in the direction of the casino.

There was a chalet at the very end of one line. There were no lights in the windows. My companion took a key from his pocket, unlocked the door and reached out a big hand around the side, flicking on the lights. He gave me the key.

'Sleep well,' he said, uttering a faint laugh. 'And in spite of what your friend Rizzio said, I'd advise you against walking in your sleep. If you have any ideas of roaming around during the night, put them out of your mind. It can be decidedly unhealthy if someone should figure you're an intruder.'

I gave a slight nod. 'I get the picture,' I said.

'Good. Just so long as we understand each other. Mister Donero runs a nice, quiet place here. We don't like anything which could cause any embarrassment to our regular guests.'

I'm sure you don't, I thought as I

134

watched him leave, then closed and locked the door. I'd have laid odds on the roulette wheels and dice being as crooked as a corkscrew. But if the folk who came here didn't mind losing their dough that way, that was their business. All that interested me was trying to get a line on Janine Jensen and whoever she came here to meet.

It wasn't going to be easy. Janine had certainly picked the best place to meet someone on the side. Donero would keep a close eye on me. Just to make sure I didn't do any straying during the night.

I switched off the lights and went to stand beside the big window.

By pressing myself as close to the wall as the wallpaper, I could just see all the way along the row of chalets, clear to the casino across the road. Occasionally, shadows passed in front of the wide doors. Twilight people, married women spending the weekend with other men, married men with other women, hidden away from the life that went on in Bay City more than fifty miles away. It was a world very few people knew about; a shadowy world where no one asked any questions just so long as you were a member.

I wished there was a way I could collect the camera and binoculars from my car but that would mean stretching my luck too far. The welcome mat Donero had grudgingly spread out for me would be pulled from under my feet within a minute.

There was a tray of fruit on the table and I'd also noticed a bottle and a fine crystal glass beside it. I picked up the bottle and glass and took them back to the window. The whisky was of the best, the kind to be savoured slowly. It was a nice touch. Maybe Donero figured that if any of his customers lost everything at the roulette or faro tables, they could at least have a good drink before shooting themselves in the head after they left. Or maybe that was just my cynical mind looking for the worst in people.

There was light coming from a couple of chalets along the row but the rest were in darkness. The roulette wheels would continue spinning throughout the night.

A couple of dark limousines drove into the distant car park. Their lights went out and more people headed for the brilliantly lit doors and the flashing neon sign. I figured hundreds of thousands of dollars would change hands in a single night, most of it going into the casino coffers and ultimately ending up in the safe in Donero's office.

I'd finished a third of the bottle when the casino doors opened and two figures emerged. I recognized Janine Jensen at once as she passed across the brilliant swathe of light pouring through the opening. Her companion deliberately stepped into the shadows.

I waited. If they intended heading for their cars and driving off into the night, I'd never get to know who this mysterious stranger was.

Then they began walking towards the road. I guessed my luck was in.

A truck with bright yellow and red lights gleaming along its sides roared past, hiding them for a moment.

Pressing my head against the wall beside the window, I held my breath.

After a moment, they crossed the road and headed towards the line of chalets. Now they were both in shadow, just anonymous shapes in the darkness.

For a couple of minutes I stood there, listening to nothing. I could only just make them out. Then they stopped outside one of the darkened chalets. There was a low murmur of conversation out of which I could make nothing. Janine inserted her key in the lock, opened the door, and went inside.

Her companion remained standing there for a few seconds, then walked on, moving across the light streaming from the window of the chalet two along from me. I recognized who it was right away.

Barbara Winton!

7

I edged back quickly along the wall, away from the window. She evidently had the chalet next to mine. A key made a tiny sound unlocking the door. I heard it close softly and then a quiet click and the light came on, spilling onto the ground outside.

I'd expected some guy to be meeting Janine. Some lover's tryst away from town, unknown to her husband. That would have made sense. But I could think of no reason for Janine to meet with Arlene's sister. I stared down at the whisky bottle in my hand, then placed it back on the table. At the moment, I needed to keep a clear head.

A radio was turned on next door. It was just loud enough for me to hear it through the dividing wall.

There was something here which just didn't add up. I figured there was only one way to get to the bottom of it. I opened the door and went outside. Through the wide window next door I could see Barbara Winton standing beside the table. She was lighting a cigarette in that elegant way of hers.

I knocked softly on the door. There was a pause. I guessed she was thinking that unless Janine had forgotten something important, no one else should be there.

Then the door opened. She stood staring at me for several seconds with a look of utter stupefaction on her beautiful features. She recovered her composure almost immediately.

'Mister Merak! What on earth are you doing here?'

'Slumming,' I said. 'May I come in?'

She considered that, then stepped to one side. I went in. Leaning past me, she threw a quick glance along the row of chalets, then closed the door. Her perfume drifted past me in a cloud of fragrance. The expression on her face told me nothing. She could have been very angry, puzzled, or even scared by my presence.

She ran her tongue around her lips,

then said, 'This isn't the kind of place I'd expect you to frequent. Do you know how much it costs to stay in one of these chalets, just for one night?'

'I wouldn't like to guess,' I said.

'Then how did you do it? I doubt if your business generates sufficient money for even such a brief vacation.'

'True,' I remarked. 'But there are times when it pays to have rich and influential people at your back.'

'Charles Jensen.'

I shook my head. 'I doubt if Jensen even knows this place exists. Even if he does, I don't think his name would have got me in here.'

'Then who?'

'Just a friend. His name wouldn't mean anything to you.'

She let that pass. I could see it didn't really interest her who had backed me. What did interest her was why I was there.

'How did you know I was here?' she asked. 'I presume you followed me from L.A.'

'I didn't. Believe me, this is as much of

a surprise to me as I must be to you.'

She walked across to the low divan and sat down, crossing her legs casually. Blowing a cloud of smoke into the air, she said, 'Then why are you here?'

'Business,' I told her. 'Nothing to do with what you hired me to look into, I'm afraid. I just spotted you out there and came to give my condolences on what happened to your sister. It must have come as a terrible shock, believing she died four years ago, only to find out she'd been murdered only a few days ago.'

Her eyes narrowed a shade. It took some of the beauty from her face.

'There's been some talk that you were arrested for her murder. Is that true?'

I shrugged. 'You know how it is. There are always plenty of rumours flying around like flies on a dung heap. Someone made a phone call to Lieutenant O'Leary of the L.A.P.D. I just happened to be there when your sister's body was discovered.'

Her brows went up. 'Just happened to be there?'

'That's right. I figure that whoever

142

killed her did his best to pin the murder on me.' A further thought struck me. 'I guess this means my work for you is finished. Now you know the truth, that your sister is dead, there's nothing more for me to do.'

She stubbed out her cigarette in the heart-shaped pink ashtray that looked too fragile and delicate for the job. It wouldn't have looked out of place in one of those big, glass-fronted display cabinets you always seem to find in the large houses along the ocean front.

'Sit down, Mister Merak,' she said, inclining her head towards the chair beside the table.

I sat down.

She smiled nicely at me. For the time being, all of the hardness was gone from her features. 'I think there's still a lot more you can do for me. Quite a lot.'

'I don't know how I can be of much more help now that your sister is dead. This is a police matter and I've already been warned off it by Lieutenant O'Leary and he's one guy who really means what he says.'

'I'm sure he does. I'm quite prepared to leave the catching of her killer to the police.'

'Then what more is there?' I asked.

'Just think about it. Someone must have been either hiding her, or keeping her locked up, all these years. I want you to find out who it was and where she's been.'

I reflected on what she'd said. 'You reckon then that she was being held someplace against her will?'

'That's the only logical conclusion I can come to, otherwise I'm sure she would have tried to get in contact with me. Arlene and I were very close, maybe closer than most sisters. I'm sure she would have got in touch somehow, if she'd been able to.'

I took out my pack of cigarettes, pushed one between my lips, and lit it. She moved the delicate little ashtray a little closer in my direction.

'If she was being held against her will, that could mean that whoever held her captive, also killed her,' I said.

'That was just what I was thinking.'

'But who would keep someone locked away for four years before killing them — and why?'

'Charles Jensen.'

I leaned back in the chair. Everything about this case seemed to go round and round and always end up with Charles Jensen. Certainly he had a strong motive. But why not arrange to have her killed just after the divorce? The longer she was alive, the bigger a threat she would become.

'Now why does everything have to come back to Jensen?' I asked, putting my thoughts into words.

'Can you think of anyone else who would want to kill her?' she countered. 'I can't.'

There was no immediate answer to that one. If Barbara was telling the truth, she had no call to murder her and I had no evidence which said that Janine even knew her.

'No,' I said finally, stubbing out my cigarette. 'I have to admit that either Jensen, or maybe one of his underworld colleagues, seem the logical suspects.'

Now that she had made her point, she adroitly changed the subject.

'You still haven't answered my earlier question. What brought you here tonight? The *Trocadero* is way out of your league and very few people know it even exists.'

'That's something I can't discuss.' I told her. 'Not even with you, even though I'd like to.'

She got up and turned the radio volume up a little more. There was a musing expression in her eyes. 'You don't have to tell me,' she said. 'I think I know. It wasn't me you were following. In fact, I don't think you expected to find me here. It was Janine. I should have figured it out when you told me you were working for Charles Jensen. He paid you to follow her to see who she's been meeting. It must have come as a surprise when you found out she came to meet me.'

'Has she been meeting you every time she told him she was visiting her sister?'

She turned her head slowly to look directly at me. Then she nodded.

'We do meet occasionally.'

'Do you mind telling me why?'

I didn't really expect her to answer, or if she did it would be some made-up story that was nowhere near the truth.

'I could tell you everything, Mister Merak, but it would put you in a very difficult position. I'm still your client so whatever I tell you has to be in the strictest confidence. But since you're also working for Charles Jensen, you'd have to tell him everything.'

'I get the picture,' I said. 'But when I woke up next to your sister and saw that bullet hole which made a mess of her pretty face and knew I'd been set-up, things changed a little. Whether I like it or not, somebody is out to stop me going ahead with this investigation. There've been two murders and unless this case is wrapped up pretty quickly, there are likely to be more. I don't want to be one of them.'

'Then whatever I tell you will be in strict confidence, even from your other client?'

I nodded. 'Your lawyer friend was right when he said there could be a conflict of interests if I took your case. But I guess

Jensen doesn't need to know any of this right now. When I get back to L.A. I'll just tell him I lost Janine in the dark.'

'He won't like that.' She sat down again, leaned forward and poured herself a drink.

'Just tell me what these meetings are about and leave me to worry about Charles Jensen,' I said.

Her eyes grew a little watchful, her delicately curved lips pressed tightly together. I knew she wasn't sure how far she could trust me, if at all.

Then she must have decided I was a right guy for she said, 'I've been meeting Janine on a regular basis for some time. Don't ask me how she found out about his crooked deals. She never said. But she's running scared, afraid she might go the same way as poor Arlene. She'd no idea what he was into when she first met him. Now that she knows, she wants out.'

'And she turned to you for help?'

'That's right. She knows I have someone watching every move Jensen makes. Between us, we hoped to get enough evidence to put before a grand jury. But he's clever, damnably clever.'

'I had a brief talk with that investigator you hired to watch Jensen. Seems he trailed him to Mike Corgan's place on a number of occasions. Corgan's one of the big men in the Mob. Has connections with City Hall. A useful man to know if you want to be sure of landing some lucrative building contracts.'

'He's already told me something of that,' she said.

'And have you got any real evidence?'

She shook her head. 'Nothing that would stand up in court. We know he keeps certain documents in his safe, but only he has the combination and it would be his word against ours if it ever came to a trial. That evidence which came out against Arlene, proving her adultery, was all cooked up. None of it was true.'

'I believe you,' I said. 'But isn't it risky meeting here. Donero is in thick with the underworld. And I'd say Janine is pretty well known. If she's being watched by the Mob, word is sure to get back to Jensen and both of your pretty necks will be on the block.'

'We try to be careful,' she said, her eyes still watchful. 'We chose this place because it's well out of the way.' She sipped her drink slowly.

'I just hope you're being careful enough,' I said soberly. 'You're both playing a very dangerous game.'

'No more than you are,' she replied, smiling slightly. 'You get yourself coshed, then arrested for murder, somehow talk Donero into letting you stay here.'

'Sure. But that's my business, what I get paid for. Okay, I'd like to be President but I have to settle with what I've got.'

I got up, remembering the bottle I'd left next door.

She didn't move, but a new expression came into her eyes. 'Do you have to leave?'

I grinned. 'I think I'd spoil the look of that expensive divan there if I was to sleep on it all night,' I said.

'I wasn't thinking of you spending the night on the divan,' she said, a little breathlessly.

'I know. But I gave up everything like that for Lent.'

She threw back her head and laughed softly. 'It isn't Lent now.'

'True. But what would Donero and that bruiser think if they came to my chalet to make sure I wasn't sleepwalking, found I wasn't there, and then came knocking on your door?'

She uncrossed her legs. 'I never answer my door once the lights are out.'

'I figured that. But you know what these guys are like, they never take no for an answer.'

She stood up and thrust her chin out at me. 'Do I take it that you're turning my offer down?'

'Much as I hate doing it, and I know I'll hate myself in the morning, I reckon it wouldn't be too good for business,' I said.

She moved towards the door so quickly I thought she was going to smash through it. Twisting the knob sharply, she glared at me as I brushed past her. The door slammed behind me.

Pushing open my door, I passed inside, closed the door and turned the key in the lock. I clicked on the lights. The radio next door suddenly went up a couple of notches in volume. I guess it was probably the first time in her life that Barbara Winton had been turned down like that.

I undressed and slid between the sheets. Just before I fell asleep, I told myself that maybe I was the one who'd made a fool of myself and not Barbara Winton.

8

There was no sign of either Barbara Winton or Janine the next morning. I guessed they were both keeping out of sight. I had breakfast in my chalet and then left, locking the door and taking the key to the flunkey behind the desk just to one side of the casino doors. He took it without a word and hung it on a set of hooks on the wall.

It was a little after nine and there were still a few punters at the various tables. Some looked as if they had been sitting there all night, others were obviously early morning starters hoping to make a fortune.

None of them looked at me as I walked past them towards Donero's office. I knocked and went in.

Donero was there behind the desk as if he were a permanent fixture of the place. There were several sheafs of important looking papers in front of him. One of the bouncers leaned nonchalantly against the wall to my left. He was staring closely at his hands and didn't turn his head when I walked in.

I went over and stood in front of the desk. Donero made a show of scrawling his name at the bottom of a couple of papers as if I wasn't there. Then he laid down his pen, sat back, and placed his fingertips together. He still looked as fresh as a daisy. Maybe he was a guy who didn't need any sleep.

'Well,' he said softly, 'I suppose you're now ready to leave?'

'Just as soon as I get my gun back,' I replied.

He raised his eyes slightly and smiled. It wasn't the kind of smile meant to put me at my ease. 'You never did tell me who you're working for, Merak. Could it be Sam Rizzio?'

'It could be. But it isn't. About last night, I just figured that Sam owed me a favour and he was the kind of guy with enough pull to make sure I got out of here in one piece.'

His thin lips made a hard line. 'You

obviously came here looking for someone. Maybe someone you followed from L.A.' He thought that over for a minute, then went on, 'You see, we have a duty here at the *Trocadero* to protect the interests of all our members.'

'That's very noble of you.'

Something showed briefly in his half-closed eyes but he let that pass. 'I could make you tell me.' His gaze flicked momentarily towards the guy lounging against the wall. 'There are ways, you know.'

'Sure there are, and I'm sure you know all of them. Only I figure that Rizzio might not like it and since he knows I'm here, it wouldn't be very easy to explain any sudden disappearance on my part.'

He didn't like that but I knew there was nothing he could do about it; Rizzio was too big a man to fool around with. Reaching down, he pulled open the drawer of his desk and took out my gun. He slid it across the highly polished top of the desk.

'Don't come back here, Merak.' His voice was like ice cubes tinkling into a glass. 'We're very particular about who we allow to become members.'

I tucked the gun back under my arm. It felt heavy so I knew the clip was still in it.

Donero made a slight gesture and the bouncer peeled himself away from the wall and opened the door for me. He accompanied me outside. As we walked towards the road, he said softly, 'You should count yourself lucky, Merak. Better stick to helping old ladies across the road if you want to stay healthy. Mister Donero is a bad man to cross.'

'I'll remember that,' I said.

The car park was almost full when I reached it. In spite of its isolation, the *Trocadero* clearly had a big membership and I figured that most of the members were already there.

The camera and binoculars were still on the passenger seat where I'd left them. Sliding behind the wheel, I switched on the ignition and drove out onto the hill road. There was very little traffic until I hit the outskirts of town. All the way I tried to figure out what I was going to tell Charles Jensen. He probably wouldn't get in touch until Monday morning, reckoning I'd still be out keeping a close tail on Janine.

Whatever I told him, it would have to be good. He wasn't the kind of man to be fobbed off with feeble excuses.

As it happened, I didn't have to think up any. No sooner had I parked the car and entered my apartment than the phone rang. It had an urgent ring about it and I guessed before I picked it up that there was some kind of trouble.

It was O'Leary. He didn't sound too pleased. 'Where the hell have you been, Merak? I've been trying to get hold of you for the past couple of hours.'

'I've been out,' I said. 'I don't usually work Saturdays.'

'Maybe some guys don't,' he snapped. 'But some of us do. I want you over at Jensen's place right away. You got that?'

'I've got it, Lieutenant. But I — '

'Just be there.' The phone went dead.

I did as I was told. It was easy playing smart with guys like Donero, but O'Leary was a different matter. When he said he wanted you someplace, it was wise to do as he said.

This time the big iron gates were wide open when I drove up. I turned the Merc into the wide drive and stopped just outside the front door. There were a couple of patrol cars parked on the drive and just as I got out, an ambulance drove up behind me.

There was no sign of O'Leary but less than a minute later he came through the front door. He spotted me standing there and hurried over.

'All right, Merak,' he said thinly. 'You finally made it. Come with me. This you've got to see.'

I fell into step beside him, wondering what was coming next. He led the way through the house and then out of the door at the back. There was a long veranda running along one side of the building. It had a glass roof to let in the summer sun but it was no longer in pristine condition.

There was a ragged, gaping hole at the far end with large shards of glass strewn across the floor.

There was also something else. Charles

Jensen lay there, face down, and there was blood all over the place. One side of his head was a mess.

An arm was flung out to one side, the fingers clenched into a tight ball.

The other arm was twisted beneath him. He had on a white shirt and pale cream trousers and his face wore an expression of utter surprise. It wasn't the look of a man who'd thought everything over carefully and decided there was only one way out.

'We figure he fell from that window up there,' O'Leary said. He pointed.

Through the wide hole in the glass I stared up at the window he indicated. It was at least forty feet above the ground.

'Fell? Or was he pushed?'

O'Leary straightened. 'Good question. Until I know a lot more, I'd say he was either pushed or thrown. He wasn't the kind of man who'd just jump. From what I gather so far, his business was in good shape. No hint of any financial trouble.'

'Who found him?' I asked.

'One of the servants. He heard the

crash, came out, and found him lying there.'

'What time was that?'

O'Leary gave me a sharp look. 'I'm the one asking the questions. But if you want to know, about a couple of hours ago.'

'So why bring me into it? Unless you figure I killed him.'

'The thought never crossed my mind.' He turned and led the way back into the house. 'We already have our chief suspect. His wife. She's nowhere to be found although the servants say she left last night around seven and she hasn't been seen since. The way I see it, she parked up somewhere close by, came back, and killed him. Now she could be anywhere but I've got word out to pick her up. Shouldn't be too difficult.'

'I can make it easy for you, Lieutenant. I know exactly where she is.'

He stopped short at that and swung round to face me. The suspicious look was back in his eyes. 'How do you know where she is?'

'Jensen hired me to follow her whenever she left on these weekend jaunts. She told him she was visiting her sister in Cleveland but he figured she was meeting some other guy. So I followed her when she left last night. She drove over a hundred miles into the country to a casino called the *Trocadero*. Far as I know, she spent the entire night there. If she keeps to the pattern, she'll still be there until Monday morning.'

'You're not making a good job of keeping an eye on her then. Why are you here if she's still there?'

'That's a long story, Lieutenant. A difference of opinion between me and the casino owner.'

O'Leary looked a shade disappointed. 'So you followed her to this casino. Even if it is a hundred miles away, she could still have slipped out sometime during the night without anyone seeing her, driven here, parked the car out of sight, then let herself in and killed him.

'Plenty of time for her to drive back to that place and be there by the time I put a call through. You can't guarantee she was there all night.'

'No, I guess not. I don't think she's the

kind of dame who'd invite me into her bed for the night, not even to give herself a watertight alibi.'

His lips twisted into what was meant to be a smile but it looked false.

We went up two flights of stairs and into a room on the left. There were a couple of officers there making a detailed examination and a fingerprint man was dusting the window. They glanced round briefly as we entered and then went on with their work.

I'd figured it for a bedroom, but it wasn't. It was fitted out as an office. There was the biggest mahogany desk I'd ever seen on one side with elegantly carved legs like tree trunks. It must have taken an army of men to have got it up there. Several bookcases lined the walls and a gleaming white telephone stood on the desk.

I turned my attention to the window. The ledge was at least four feet from the floor and the window was wide open.

'I suppose you've taken a good look at that window, Lieutenant,' I said.

'Sure. What about it?'

162

'Doesn't it strike you as odd that it's wide open? Okay, so it gets warm through the night but not enough to open it all the way. And the ledge is far too high for anyone to just topple over.'

'Unless they were so drunk they didn't know what they were doing.'

'Which is hardly likely at that time of the morning. From what I saw of him, Jensen wasn't the kind to turn to the bottle that early in the day.'

'So what are you saying? He was definitely murdered?'

'I'd say there's no doubt about it. The way I see it, the killer was someone Jensen knew because there's no sign of any struggle. If I'd wanted to kill him, I'd hit him with a sap on the side of the head, drag him to the window and heave him over the ledge. That way he'd hit the ground head first and it would wipe out any evidence of a scalp wound.'

O'Leary looked at me poker-faced. 'So we're agreed it had to be someone he knew.'

'I reckon so. You've seen these houses. They're all like Fort Knox. It wouldn't be easy for a total stranger to get in. But I figure this lets Janine off the hook.'

'How so?'

'I met Jensen about a week ago when he came to my office. I'd say he was a couple of inches taller than me, weight around two twenty-five, kept himself in good shape with weekly visits to the gym. Do you reckon Janine could have dragged him across the floor and then lifted him over that ledge?'

O'Leary forced a smile. 'Maybe, maybe not. Perhaps she went to the gym as often as he did.'

'Okay,' I said. 'You win. But I still think you've got the wrong suspect.'

'We'll see once we bring her in for questioning.' He pushed his hat further back on his head. 'What did you say the name of this casino is?'

'The *Trocadero*,' I told him. 'It's way out along the coast highway heading north. You take a turn-off onto a hill road. It's pretty remote.'

'And the guy who runs this place?'

'His name's Donero. My guess is that he's a big man with one of the mobs.'

O'Leary nodded. 'I've heard the name somewhere. But wherever it is, that place is out of my territory.' He pulled his lips together into a tight line. 'Even if she is innocent, we'll have to get in touch with her.'

There was a guy bending over the body when we got back down into the veranda. He straightened up as O'Leary walked over.

I recognized him as Doctor Venner. He usually did the autopsies for the cops in cases like this. He was a quiet man in his fifties, soberly dressed except for a flamboyant tie that was a brilliant emerald with deep scarlet stripes running diagonally across it. I felt dizzy just looking at it.

'Got anything for me, Doc?' O'Leary asked.

'Not much at the moment, Lieutenant. Dead for a couple of hours I'd say. No doubt what killed him. He must have died as soon as he hit the ground.'

'Any evidence he might have been hit on the head before he fell?'

Venner pursed his lips. 'That's possible,

I suppose. You're treating this as murder?'

'For the moment — yes.'

Venner didn't look surprised. He had that kind of stone face that never looked surprised at anything. 'It'll need a more detailed examination before I can answer that. When can he be removed?'

'Just as soon as the photographers have done their job. Then he's all yours.'

O'Leary took out a handkerchief and mopped his face. He glanced in my direction. 'I won't be needing you for anything more, Merak,' he said. 'And as you can see, your late client won't be requiring your services either.' The way he said it made it sound as if he was almost pleased I'd just lost a lucrative job.

'Maybe Mrs. Jensen might be in need of them,' I said. 'If she does, I'm sure she'll know where to find me.'

'I wouldn't bet on it,' he retorted acidly.

I climbed into the Merc, lit a cigarette, and leaned back in the seat. First his ex-wife after a long and mysterious disappearance, and now Jensen.

More coincidence?

I didn't think so. There was a dark thread of cause and effect running through this case. What made me so sure the same person had killed them both — and Ricardo — I didn't know. The way I figured it, Arlene had been killed because she knew too much. Jensen may have been silenced because he was getting scared of the men he was working with and wanted out.

Either way, it looked like the Mob had had a hand in it somewhere. All three killings had the look of the professional about them. From what I'd seen, it wasn't going to be as easy as O'Leary thought to prove that Jensen hadn't committed suicide. It was only O'Leary's and my suspicious minds that had jumped at the possibility of cold-blooded murder.

I finished the cigarette and flipped the butt out of the window and watched it burn down to the very end on the gravel. Compared to the mess in the verandah, one cigarette butt on the immaculate drive didn't amount to much.

I drove back to my apartment and made myself something to eat. While I ate, I tried to visualize what was going on at that moment. Jensen's body would be taken to the morgue for further examination by Venner.

O'Leary would be on the phone to the *Trocadero* to try to trace Janine.

I didn't doubt she'd have an iron-cast alibi but that wouldn't put him off. Maybe, of course, she had planned it all, right down to the last little detail. Maybe she'd even guessed someone would be following her and had made damned sure I trailed her all the way to the *Trocadero*. From what I'd seen of the place it would be quite simple for her to leave her chalet without being seen. Everyone else would be inside the big gaming room trying to pit themselves against the crooked wheels and loaded dice.

Once in her car, she'd drive out onto that fairly quiet road, not putting on her lights until she was at least a couple of miles away. Then she could have done exactly as O'Leary had worked out. Parked in some quiet street not far from the house, let herself in, found him in that office on the second floor. Maybe he'd be surprised to see her but not so surprised as to be on his guard against possible murder.

A couple of hard blows on the side of the head would be enough to render him unconscious. Then all she had to do was drag him across the floor, lift him over the ledge, and the rest would be up to gravity.

Getting out of the house unnoticed would be even easier than getting in with all of the servants milling around outside once Charles' body was discovered. Then a fast drive back to the *Trocadero* and her alibi would be as secure as the National Deposit.

Every little piece fitted together so nicely and exactly, it was almost impossible to find a flaw in it. But those little mice inside my head weren't lying down nice and quiet. Instead, they were running around, telling me there was something wrong. That gut-feeling in my stomach that the same person had committed all three murders, was still there, as strong as ever.

And that was where the flaw in my theory was. Janine had two of the most powerful motives for killing her husband; fear and money. As his widow, she stood to gain far more than she'd ever get in alimony.

But why would she kill Arlene?

In spite of what I'd told O'Leary, I didn't really expect to see Janine Jensen again. I heard she'd been taken in for questioning but she had a couple of slick city lawyers who got several people to claim she was at the *Trocadero* during the time her husband had been killed. Barbara Winton's name wasn't mentioned. But then, I figured, it wouldn't be. She wasn't supposed to even know Janine.

O'Leary would have loved to have her charged with first-degree murder if he could. But with insufficient evidence he had to let her go.

The following Wednesday and I'd spent most of the time checking with the few contacts I had in the L.A. underworld, trying to find out where Arlene had been during the four years before her death. Nobody seemed to know anything. Either they weren't talking, or they really knew nothing.

I was running through my mental notes to see if there was anyone else I could call when the phone rang.

I picked it up, expecting it to be O'Leary. It wasn't. Barbara Winton's clear, cool tones said, 'Is that you, Mister Merak?'

'The same,' I said. 'What can I do for you?'

'I'd like to see you. It's important — and urgent.'

'Where are you? I understood you were going back home at the weekend. I figured that meeting with Janine Jensen was some sort of farewell party.'

'Now you're being facetious.' She uttered a faint chuckle. 'Unfortunately, I've had to change all of my plans. I'm still at the *Drayton* and likely to be here for some time. I think you know the room number.'

'Two twenty-four,' I said.

'I guess you were always good with figures.'

'Some figures I like better than others. May I ask if this has anything to do with

Charles Jensen's rather sudden and unfortunate demise?'

Her voice went as cold as yesterday's dinner. 'I'll explain everything when I see you. There are some things it's not wise to discuss over the phone.'

'If you say so.'

'I do say so.' Her tone was now so hard you could have broken an ice pick on it. 'Can I expect you within half an hour?'

'I'll be ringing your bell before you put the phone down,' I said.

This time, the guy outside the door of the *Drayton* allowed me through without any questions. Obviously, he was a man who never forgot a face. I went up in the silent elevator. The same bruiser was there reading the same newspaper. He didn't even look up when I knocked softly on the door.

Another guy with a photogenic memory, I decided. Where Barbara Winton got him from I didn't know.

The door opened and I went in. The room was exactly as I remembered it. It was like a repeat from a scene in one of the old movies. Except this time there was someone else apart from Barbara and her lawyer friend.

Janine Jensen sat at the other end of the elegant divan from Barbara. She looked tensed and scared and kept twisting her fingers together in her lap.

I studied her closely without seeming to. Her hair was real blonde with no hint anywhere of any other color than that of ripe corn. She had a figure full of curves, all in the right places.

'Mrs. Jensen,' I said. 'I was wondering when we might meet.'

She didn't look the kind who would kill her husband in cold blood.

She didn't look the kind who'd squash a bug even if it got beneath her dainty foot. But in spite of her little girl lost expression I had the feeling that, underneath, she was as hard as nails.

'I asked Janine to come here because I'm hoping you can help her,' Barbara said, 'I'm sure that in our two cases there'll be no conflict of interests. Basically, we both want the same thing.'

'I can understand that,' I said. 'But I don't know whether I can do anything.

There's really nothing to go on. All of the leads I thought I might have now turn out to be dead ends.'

'I'm sure you can help if you really try,' Barbara turned her head and glanced sideways at Janine. 'She already knows that you followed her to the *Trocadero*.'

I sat down in the chair she indicated and waited while the big guy, silent as the Sphinx, poured me a drink.

I took a sip of the bourbon and stared at Janine over the rim of the glass. 'Do you know why I followed you?' I asked.

She nodded and the long blonde curls danced delightfully around her shoulders. 'I believe my husband — I mean my late husband — hired you to follow me.'

'He did. He thought you were having an adulterous affair with some other man. At least, that's what he told me. He wanted pictures, taped conversations, the lot.'

'And now you know it was me she was meeting all the time,' Barbara put in. She seemed to be doing all the talking for the two of them. It made me wonder whether that was because Janine was still in shock, or she was afraid her companion might say something out of turn.

'Since we're all confessing our sins,' she went on soberly, 'I think there's something you should know. It's probably been bothering you for some time. The mystery woman who warned you off taking Jensen's case and then took a shot at you. It wasn't Arlene — it was me.'

'Huh?' I said, surprised. It was something I hadn't seriously considered before.

'I was afraid that if you started sniffing around, you might discover that Janine and I have been working together, trying to get the lowdown on Charles. I had to do something, so I borrowed Janine's car that night. You were never in any real danger. I'm an excellent shot, even in the dark. Believe me, if I'd meant to kill you, you wouldn't be sitting here now.'

I swallowed a little more of my drink. 'Okay, so that clears up one thing that's been niggling at me. If it had been your sister and someone had been keeping her holed up for four years, why should they let her out just to warn me off? All she had to do was get into that car and take off for parts unknown. And they'd never have given her a loaded gun to play with.'

'So we've cleared up that little mystery. Now, are you willing to help my friend here?'

I swung my gaze to Janine, still fidgeting with her hands. 'I'd like to hear what you have to say, Mrs. Jensen. Up to now this has been more like a ventriloquist act than a conversation.'

'You don't have to be insulting,' Barbara said acidly. 'Can't you see that she's still shocked by what has happened?'

'I fully understand that,' I said, speaking directly to Janine. 'But if I'm to be of any help to you, I have to know everything and you're the only one who can tell me.'

Her full lips twisted a little and I thought I detected tears in her eyes. 'I didn't kill my husband. You've got to believe that. I wasn't even there when it happened but that detective seems determined to pin it on me.'

'But you do know that he was mixed up

with some pretty shady characters.'

She hesitated. Her glance flicked towards Barbara who nodded slightly.

'I suspected it. I wasn't sure at first. Then I found this.' She dug inside her expensive handbag and took something out. She handed it to me. It was a cheque book. Charles' cheque book.

'You'll see there are several cheques for large amounts, all of them apparently made out to the same person.'

I riffled through the stubs and soon saw what she was getting at. I counted fifteen, all for the same amount — two hundred and fifty thousand dollars. At the top of each stub, just below the date, was scrawled the letters MC.

I handed the cheque book back. 'I'd say this is dynamite, especially if it fell into the wrong hands,' I said.

Her face whitened perceptibly beneath the faint powdering of rouge. 'You know what those letters stand for?'

'Sure. I'd say they stand for Mike Corgan. He's a gangster, a big name in the Mob. Your husband was in the habit of visiting him at fortnightly intervals and

I don't think they're poker debts. He was paying Corgan to get him in with City Hall who hand out big building contracts all over town.'

She tried to put a brave face on things and failed miserably. 'Then you think this man Corgan could have killed Charles?'

I shrugged. 'It's possible, of course. Anything's possible. But I doubt it. These guys like money first and power second. It wouldn't be like Corgan to kill the goose that laid the golden eggs. From those stubs, I'd say your late husband was keeping up the payments on a regular basis. The Mob like that. So long as he stayed in business, they'd go along with him. They'd only resort to murder if he tried to double-cross them.'

I swallowed the rest of my drink, held the glass out as the silent man moved forward like a shadow and took it from me. It came back refilled within fifteen seconds.

'Just what do you figure on doing now, Mrs. Jensen?' I asked. 'About the business, I mean. As his wife, I presume everything goes to you.'

'Don't you think it's a little early to ask questions like that?' Barbara demanded. 'Her husband has only been dead three days. He's not even buried. She hasn't had any time to think.'

'I'm sorry. But as your lawyer friend here will tell you, she has some very tough decisions to make — and fast. And if she makes the wrong ones, it could be very dangerous.'

Barbara looked puzzled. 'In what way?'

'These hoodlums who were behind Charles Jensen won't wait for long. I don't suppose you'll want to keep the business and run it yourself, Mrs. Jensen?'

She shook her head. 'I don't know the first thing about the construction business. Charles had a number of associates who worked for him. Perhaps one of them — '

I shrugged and drank.

The lawyer spoke up for the first time. 'If Mrs Jensen wants my advice, I'm sure one of the other big firms in L.A. would be willing to buy her out at a very good price.'

'That's true,' I acknowledged. 'But unfortunately you have Mike Corgan and his associates to consider. Unless you get their say-so, I think you'll find it very difficult to get anyone else interested. And if your possession of that cheque book should become known by anyone outside this room — '

Janine looked as though she was on the verge of breaking down.

Barbara's expression was unreadable. Then she said sharply, 'We'll cross that bridge when we come to it. In the meantime, is there anything you can do to help us find her husband's killer and take the heat off her?'

'That's strictly a police matter,' I told her. 'And they don't take too kindly to people like me meddling in their cases.'

She snorted derisively. It suddenly made her seem unladylike. 'I doubt if that's bothered you in the past. And you know the police won't look any further than Janine. As far as they're concerned, they've got their killer and it's only a matter of time before they dredge up some trumped-up evidence and make this murder rap stick.'

What she said was probably true. O'Leary wasn't going to waste time looking for anyone else. Certainly, he wouldn't entertain the possibility that it was a mob killing.

Janine bit her lower lip. 'This gangster Corgan — do you know him?'

'Only slightly, by reputation. He's not someone to play around with. You may not know it, but it's very easy for these men to buy themselves a piece of this town. They have their fingers in everything that makes money, gambling saloons, honky-tonks, all-night bars. Why do you ask?'

'I'd thought of going to the police with this evidence but now I don't think that would be a very good idea.'

'It wouldn't. They'd just say it proves that Corgan had no motive for killing Charles. They'd most likely toss it into the bin and forget about it. And it wouldn't be long before Corgan knew all about it.'

'But you must have had contact with these men in the past. Perhaps if you went to see Corgan and — '

'Now hold on a minute, lady.' I said. 'I've taken some big chances in my time but if Corgan was even to guess I knew about his involvement, I'd find myself lying face up with my neck on the block, watching the blade coming down. I've already had a run-in with Donero and only got out of it by the skin of my teeth. Even if I could get near Corgan, which is a very big if, what do I tell him?'

'You could tell him you're representing Janine and you're wondering what his reaction would be if she decided to sell the business,' Barbara said.

'Wouldn't that be better coming from your lawyer friend here?' I looked across at the guy now standing near the window. He seemed to be watching the street below and taking no interest in the proceedings inside the room.

I knew he'd never even consider such a proposal. He was a man who dealt only with the higher-class, upright citizens of L.A. Guys like Corgan were so far beneath him they were almost out of sight. Besides, they were known to carry guns and use them whenever the occasion demanded. He'd probably never fired a gun in his life and would be appalled if one were pointed in his direction.

'Five thousand dollars for you if you do this little favour for us,' Barbara said sweetly. I looked at her. I'd never known a woman who could change from being acid to sweet in so short a time.

I thought it over. I could see she knew I was interested, if not for the dough, for the chance of nailing Jensen's killer before O'Leary did.

Finally, I said, 'Okay, I'll do it. But I can't promise anything.'

'I'm sure you'll do your very best,' she said. She motioned to the bouncer. I picked up my hat and went out, quite sure I'd just made the biggest mistake of my life.

9

Once I left the *Drayton*, I figured there was no time like the present to start earning that five thousand dollars. The little guy Barbara had hired to follow Jensen had said he'd visited an address on Bay Avenue to meet Corgan. It was off Sunset, away from the ocean, filled with all-night dance halls, casinos, bars and any other place of dubious 'entertainment' you cared to mention.

Most of these places still paid protection money to stay in business. Occasionally, one would be raided by the cops just to show the world they were still on the ball. A couple of days later, after paying their fine, they would be back in business.

I didn't have the number of the address but I reckoned Corgan wouldn't be a hard man to find. Whether he'd consider talking to me was a different matter. I did, however, have one trump card in my hand. If he'd had no hand in it, he'd be just as concerned over Jensen's death as Janine. And if what I'd picked up was true, he'd had a big stake in Jensen's construction empire and he'd want that to continue.

There were only a couple of cars parked along the avenue and one of them was a big, flashy Cadillac, not the kind your ordinary citizen would acquire in a lifetime of honest toil. It was parked directly outside the Bay Casino. I drew into the kerb a little way behind it and got out.

There was a tall, thin guy standing just outside the door, leaning nonchalantly against the wall, a half-smoked cigarette dangling from his lower lip. He was looking at nobody in particular.

He barely moved as I walked along the dusty sidewalk and stopped right in front of him. His eyes were half-closed, kind of glazed, and I guessed that whatever it was he was smoking, it had never grown on a tobacco plant.

'Mike Corgan in?' I asked.

One eye widened fractionally. He tried

to look as if he didn't know the name.

'Who?' The question was a throaty rasp.

'Mike Corgan. I reckon he owns this joint.'

The other eye opened wider. 'What's your racket? A cop?'

'Now why do I have to tell you?' I said. 'If Mike is in, just tell him I'm from Janine Jensen. He'll understand.'

The disinterested expression faded slightly from his face. Maybe he had me figured for an undercover cop, after all. Then he eased himself from the wall and went inside, disappearing into the steamy dimness just inside the door.

I waited. I felt just like Daniel before stepping into the lion's den.

Five minutes and then he came out again. He looked at me oddly as if I'd just popped up out of the sidewalk. Then he jerked a grimy thumb towards the door. 'Mister Corgan's office is at the end of the passage and up the stairs. He's expecting you.'

'Somehow, I thought he would be,' I said as I brushed past him. A whiff of white smoke stung the back of my nostrils. I knew that my guess about his smoking habits had been correct.

For a few seconds, it was impossible for me to see anything inside the place after the glare of sunlight in the street. Then the dancing green haze slowly drifted away. I made out the narrow passage in front of me. There was an open door to my right. Beyond it was a big room, the walls lined with gaming machines, the middle occupied by three roulette tables. It was the *Trocadero* only on a much smaller and shabbier scale.

The passage continued for a further twenty yards or so and ended at a flight of stairs. I went up them to the closed door at the top. I knocked. A voice called something from inside. Pushing the door open, I stepped through. The room was bigger than I expected. Smoke hung like cobwebs in the air and it had the same smell as that which I'd met at the street door.

Three guys sat around the long table in the middle. The only light came from a couple of dirty bulbs near the ceiling but it was just bright enough for me to make out details. I recognized two of the hoods right away. Ed Marcos and Slim Fenton, both close associates of the Big Man, Manzelli. I guessed the third was Mike Corgan.

He was thin, almost to the point of gauntness, straight as a steel rod, with coal black hair slicked back and parted in the middle. His brows were thick and of the same color. But it was his eyes that caught, and held, my attention. Milk-white, they never moved. I knew at once that he was blind.

I didn't know why, but the realization sent a little shiver down my spine. You can usually tell what someone is thinking by looking at their eyes. But in his case there was nothing there, just a white emptiness.

There was a gun on the table within easy reach of his right hand. I wondered if he ever used it.

'I understand you wish to see me,' he said. His voice was cultured and held a trace of accent that I couldn't place. 'Would you identify yourself?'

'My name's Merak. I'm a private investigator.'

'Then either you are a very brave man or a very stupid one. Since there are very few brave men around, I have to suppose that you're stupid.'

'All right,' I said. 'So I'm stupid. Then why did you agree to see me?'

'Curiosity, perhaps. You say you represent Mrs. Jensen. May I ask what she has to do with me?'

'Well, now that Jensen is dead, I guess she really does take command of his business empire.'

'You didn't come here just to tell me that, I'm sure. Besides, from what I've heard, the cops have already fingered her for the murder. She won't be in a position to control anything from a prison cell.'

There was an empty chair at the table, facing Corgan. I pulled it out and sat down. The lustreless eyes swivelled slightly. In spite of his blindness, he knew exactly, to the inch, where I was.

'If you've got anything more to tell me, Merak, then spill it,' Marcos said gratingly. 'Otherwise you're wasting our time.'

I sat forward on the edge of the chair, my elbows on the table, trying to act less nervous than I was. 'I'm talking about Charles Jensen, about a rendezvous he kept every other Friday night, about an address he visited. My guess is that he didn't come here so the four of you could play a few friendly hands of gin rummy. There's millions of dollars at stake here and I reckon you don't want to miss out on your slice just because Jensen gets himself killed and his wife takes the helm.'

The expression on Corgan's face didn't alter. Not even a muscle twitched. But my words had clearly hit home.

'You followed him here?' he asked coolly.

'Not me. Some other private dick. Now if Mrs. Jensen decides to sell the business, she'll end up a very rich woman. More to the point, depending upon the buyer, you stand to lose quite a lot. Somehow, I don't think Manzelli would like that.'

'So what's your interest in all this?' Corgan's right hand moved half an inch closer to the gun in front of him. 'Don't tell me you're her knight in shining armour trying to protect her against the big, bad world.'

'Not exactly,' I said. 'But I'm damned sure she didn't kill her husband. Furthermore, I reckon I can talk her into disposing of the business in a way which would be advantageous to you.'

'And what would you want out of it, always assuming that we're already interested?'

'Jensen was my client. You have contacts that I don't. I want you to help me track down his killer — and one other thing.'

'Go on.'

'Someone kept Arlene Jensen, his first wife, hidden away for four years, then killed her and tried to pin the murder on me. I want to know who kept her and where she was hidden all that time.'

Corgan ran his tongue slowly around his lips. 'You think they were both mob killings? I'm not suggesting they were and I've heard of no hitmen being involved.'

Both Marcos and Fenton shook their heads in unison.

Corgan spread his hands on the table. So far, he'd made no move towards picking up the gun. 'Personally, I can see no reason for anyone wanting to get rid of Jensen, except for his wife. As for his ex-wife, why should we want to hide her? She was of no interest to us.'

He leaned back and stared at me, if it was possible for a blind man to stare at anything. I couldn't tell what thoughts were running through his head at that moment.

Then he said softly, 'I don't make you out at all, Merak. I've heard of you. I know you were instrumental in bringing the killer of Carlos Galecci to justice. Now you risk your neck to come here, knowing you could very easily vanish through the back door of this club and no one would be any the wiser. But I'll admit that your offer of talking to Janine Jensen and making sure she doesn't make the wrong decision, appeals to me. And we can always find you if you should decide to double-cross us and talk to the cops.'

'Then do we have a deal?' I asked.

He sat perfectly still for more than a

minute. It was as if he were communing telepathically with his two confederates.

At last, he said, 'I'm not promising anything. I don't like working with men like you, you're too close to the police for my liking. But you took a big chance coming here so this is what I'll do. I'll spread the word around about this Arlene Jensen and let you know what I pick up. In return, I'll let you have a list of names we'd support as suitable buyers if Jensen's widow agrees to sell.'

'That's fine by me,' I said. I knew that if O'Leary got to know about this deal he'd throw the book at me, lock me up, and toss away the key.

I glanced at the three of them in turn. None of them said anything more and I guessed that the meeting was at an end.

I scraped back my chair and got up. Corgan's right hand still rested within an inch of the gun. All the way to the door, I could feel those sightless eyes boring into my back. Even though he couldn't see me, he knew exactly where I was every step of the way.

I opened the door and slipped out,

closing it softly behind me. I could feel the sweat on the back of my neck and between my shoulders.

The lookout was still holding up the wall outside. He looked at me out of the corner of one half-closed eye. The look in it seemed one of surprise that I was able to walk out of there on my own two feet.

'You see Corgan?' he drawled.

'Sure, I saw him,' I said. 'He seems a pretty reasonable sort of guy.'

I left him staring after me and climbed into the Merc. I had the feeling I'd just committed an offence that was going to land me in big trouble. I could see my licence to practise already disappearing fast over the horizon. It wasn't a nice feeling.

The big Cadillac was still there dozing in the sun, no doubt waiting to transport Corgan to another of his establishments in town. I hoped the guy lounging outside the door wasn't his driver. The state he was in, I doubted if he could see clearly across the street.

I decided to take the country road back to the other side of town. It would be much quieter that way and I needed to do some serious thinking before I got back to the office. I was sticking my neck out for Janine getting in with hoods like Corgan. If things didn't go the way he wanted, I might not live to pick up my five grand from Barbara Winton.

It was another hot day but there was a breeze blowing off the sea and that cooled down things a little.

I started the car and drove out past the Cadillac. The street was virtually empty. A kid was kicking a can along the sidewalk but that was all. Glancing in the mirror, I looked to see if Corgan or any of his cronies had decided to tail me. They hadn't but another car, parked several yards behind the spot where I'd been, suddenly pulled out.

That started me thinking. Maybe Corgan wasn't all that sure he could trust me and had put a tail on me. Maybe it was just some guy going about his legitimate business. But I didn't like 'maybes'. I like cold, hard facts. I decided the only way to get the facts was to let him follow me and not put too many difficulties in his way.

I deliberately drove all the way to the city outskirts and then on into the country. Here the roads were quiet as I'd expected, quiet enough for him to keep me in sight and make his move if he had something on his mind. The road curved away in front of me, dozing quietly and peacefully in the sun. The heat made the surface dance like smoke on water.

A couple of heavy trucks passed me on the other side and my shadow remained a steady distance behind. I put my foot down slightly and eased the Merc up to fifty. Whoever was tailing me did the same.

I turned east onto the road leading back towards L.A. It ran in a long curve, turning south where it led into town less than fifteen minutes from my office. A long, easy drive where nothing can happen. Only whoever was tailing me suddenly got other ideas.

Without any warning, he put his foot down, roaring up on me from behind. I had only enough time to realize what he intended when his front fender rammed the Merc in the back. The car jumped forward like a horse that had been stung on the rump.

Somehow, I managed to hold onto the wheel and suck air back into my lungs. Ten seconds and the same thing happened again. I tried to keep control of the car and peer into the rear mirror at the same time. Whoever was driving that car certainly didn't intend being recognized.

He had something over his face, something dark with holes cut into it for eyes. Gritting my teeth, I pushed the accelerator to the floor. The Merc may have taken a battering in its long lifetime but there was still plenty of power beneath the hood.

Ten seconds and the needle stood at eighty. For a moment, I thought I might lose him. He dropped behind for perhaps a hundred yards. Then he came on again. This time, he changed his tactics, pulling out and drawing alongside me. Out of the corner of my eye I saw him turn his head briefly, staring at me through the window. I couldn't see any more. The balaclava he was wearing covered his face completely. He must have been sweating ice cubes inside that mask.

Swinging the wheel, he slammed into the side of the Merc, trying to force me off the road. I gripped the wheel as if my hands were welded to it and somehow managed to keep the car on an even keel. Another jar that rattled my bones like dice bouncing across a crap table. Swinging my gaze back to the road ahead, I saw the sharp bend coming up fast and there was something else. A big freight truck cruising at a steady fifty, all chrome and steel gleaming brilliantly in the harsh sunlight.

The guy in the car must have seen it a split second later. He only had a couple of seconds in which to make up his mind what he was going to do. He did — and made his last big mistake. He must have figured he couldn't be sure of accelerating past me in time. He did what I reckoned he would do, he slammed on his brakes to get in behind me.

I did the last thing he expected. I braked as well, matching my speed with his, giving him no chance of slipping in behind me. The truck was less than twenty feet away when I accelerated. In the mirror I saw him wrestling desperately with the wheel as he tried to turn out of the path of the truck.

He almost made it. Then, a wheel as big as a mountain smashed into the rear of the car. It was like a baseball bat swatting a fly. I glimpsed the car jump a dozen feet into the air to perform a perfect somersault before hitting the embankment and rolling down the side.

Stopping the car, I got out and walked back. The truck driver, a guy in his forties and built like the truck he was driving, was already there, staring wide-eyed down the slope.

'What the hell was that crazy fool trying to do — kill himself?' His voice quavered just a little. 'Pulling out like that across the road.'

'It wasn't your fault,' I told him. 'Have you got any way to contact the cops and an ambulance in your cab?'

'Sure.'

'Then I suggest you do it right away. I'll

try to get down there and see if there's anything I can do for him.'

I waited until the driver ran back to his truck before working my way down the steep incline. The car lay on its side, wedged tightly against a ledge of rock. The rear was just a tangled mess but the front seemed to have only sustained damage from the fall. I first checked the gasoline tank but that seemed to be still intact so there was little chance of me being roasted in a fire.

Then I inched my way round to the front. The driver was slumped sideways behind the wheel and he wasn't moving. Somehow, I wrenched the door open. There was blood coming from beneath one side of the hood he wore and I guessed he had also sustained internal injuries from hitting the wheel.

Easing him back, I gently pulled the balaclava over his head and tossed it outside onto the ground. I reckoned he was somewhere in his mid-thirties and I didn't recognize the face. I was disappointed. I'd hoped that, since he'd gone to all the trouble and discomfort of masking his identity, he was someone I should know.

Reaching down, I started to search through his pockets, trying to move him as little as possible. There was nothing, not even a driver's licence. Whoever he was, he'd made damned sure there was nothing on him to give a clue to his identity. If I'd needed anything to tell me he was a hitman and I'd been his target, that was it.

I left him where he was and climbed back up to the road. The truck driver was already there, waiting for me. 'The cops and an ambulance should be here in a few minutes,' he said. He was still white-faced under the tan and shaking a little.

'I reckon he's still breathing,' I told him, hoping that might calm him down a little. 'But he's pretty badly smashed up.'

'What the hell was he doing, trying to pass you like that?'

'I've no idea,' I lied. 'Maybe he was in one hell of a hurry and didn't think what he was doing.'

'Any idea who he is?'

I shook my head. 'I've had a look

through his pockets. Nothing at all on him.'

I made to say something more but at that moment there was the wail of a police siren in the distance and a moment later, a couple of squad cars pulled up. O'Leary was in the first. His face tightened the second he saw me.

'You again, Merak,' he snarled. 'Somehow, I might have figured you would be. You seem to be haunting me.'

He walked to the edge and peered down. 'What happened?'

'He just pulled out from behind me, Lieutenant. Must have been doing close on eighty. Reckon he never saw the truck until it was too late.'

O'Leary walked back and stared at me carefully. There was a speculative gleam in his eyes.

'You're sure that's all that happened? He wouldn't have been tailing you, I suppose?'

'Now why should you think that? I've no idea who the guy is.'

'So you've already been down there and taken a look?'

'Naturally. I went down to see if there was anything I could do for him. He's still alive. I reckon if the fast-wagon gets here in time, they might even save him. I'm sure you'll want to question him.'

'If he lives.' O'Leary spoke through his teeth. 'And I'll want to talk to you later. There's something about this that stinks and my guess is that you're right in the middle of it.'

He motioned to a couple of the officers. They eased themselves over the edge and went down to the wreck.

Then he left me and took the truck driver to one side, busying himself writing down the answers to the questions he put to him. I knew there wasn't much the truck driver could tell him. What worried me was what he would think when he found that balaclava and nothing at all in the injured guy's pockets.

As it turned out, he didn't say very much. After letting the truck go on its way, he went down to join the two cops. By this time, the ambulance had arrived on the scene. It took three of them to eased him out of the car, get him onto a stretcher, and haul him up to the road. I stood beside O'Leary and watched the ambulance speed away, eating up the road into town.

Staring me straight in the eye, O'Leary said, 'That car is from outside the state. I'll run the registration number through the system but my guess is we'll not come up with anything.'

I managed to look suitably surprised. 'Then you think he was out to kill me?'

'If you didn't take anything from his pockets, there's no identification, nothing to say who he is. That hood he was probably wearing. I'd say it's pretty clear someone wants you taken out and they'll go to any lengths to do it.'

He was watching my face closely to see if anything he said struck home. I did my best to give nothing away.

'That's all,' he said after a few moments. 'You seem to be in this mess right up to your neck. If I were you, I'd watch your back from now on. And if I get a report that you've been found in some alley with a knife or a bullet in you, I won't shed any tears at your funeral.'

'Thanks for the vote of confidence, Lieutenant,' I said. I left him there, glaring after me, a scowl on his face, and walked along to my car. There were a couple of dents in the rear fender, but that was all.

Getting in, I drove back to my office.

10

I reckoned there'd be a call the next morning from O'Leary asking me to go down to the precinct and answer some awkward questions. But there wasn't. I told myself that perhaps he was waiting for the doctors' verdict on the guy who'd tried to run me off the road before calling me in.

Dawn made the coffee around ten and still the phone remained as silent as Lazarus' tomb.

Sitting on the edge of the desk, Dawn said, 'You like it the hard way, don't you, Johnny? You get in with this hoodlum Corgan like you're blood brothers — and that's a big mistake. Then you realize you're being tailed so what do you do? Try to lose him in the traffic in town? No; you deliberately take the country road so that he can run you down at his leisure with no witnesses.'

'Maybe I figured that was the only way

to find out who he was. Either he was the killer or, if these were all mob killings, he might be someone I know.'

The coffee was hot but it settled my stomach. 'Okay,' I went on, 'Someone is being very clever, bringing in a hitman from out of state to make me think the mobs are behind it.'

Dawn thought that over for a minute. 'You think that whoever the killer is, he's deliberately trying to pin it on the mobs?'

'Hell, it's just a hunch. There are more threads running through this case than in a pair of nylons.'

Dawn grinned. 'I should have said that.'

She finished her coffee and placed the cup on the desk. 'Why are you so damned pig-headed and think the mobs aren't responsible for these murders? All of the evidence you've got so far points that way. Jensen was in cahoots with them and maybe got scared and wanted out. Arlene had evidently found out they were tied in with him and had to be silenced before she could spill everything to the D.A. That crooked informer of yours was one of them. What more convincing do you need?'

'I want someone to tell me why Arlene wasn't silenced four years ago. Why she was kept somewhere all that time before being bumped off. And don't say she was kept alive just to pin her murder on me. I wasn't even remotely involved with the case at that time.'

She sighed audibly. 'So you've only two suspects now. Janine and this Barbara Winton, Arlene's sister.'

'I think we can forget Janine,' I said.

'Why? I'd say she's more likely to be the killer than Barbara Winton.' I thought I detected a brittle edge to her voice. 'Quite suddenly, she doesn't need a divorce and she's a very wealthy woman.'

I looked at her with a show of admiration. Her logic was crystal clear, impeccable.

'She fits the facts,' she said calmly. 'Certainly marking her as the killer is no more stupid than pinning it on anyone else. Suppose Arlene was blackmailing Jensen even after the divorce. It's already been rumoured in some quarters that his business was going sour and if most of his money was tied up in it, together with regular payments to his gangster colleagues, there wouldn't be as much left as Janine would have liked. It wouldn't be difficult for someone in her position to find a place where Arlene could have been kept out of sight until she was ready to kill her.

'And I don't care how many witnesses, including yourself, there are, willing to swear she was at the *Trocadero* all that night, she could have slipped back and killed her husband and then got back there before O'Leary discovered where she was.'

'It's a good theory,' I said, 'but for one thing.'

'Oh, what's that?'

'Have you ever met Janine Jensen?'

She shook her head. 'I don't see what you're getting at, Johnny.'

'I'd say about five-four, around a hundred and twenty pounds. Now Ricardo's car was parked at least a hundred yards from where Arlene was dumped beside me. You figure she could have carried her all that way? And Jensen was a big, well-built guy. So she coshed him on the side of the head, dragged him across to the window, then lifted him onto the ledge and tossed him over?'

Dawn shrugged. 'I think if the stakes are high enough, you'd be surprised just what a woman can do.'

That was when the phone rang. As I'd figured, it was O'Leary.

'I just thought I'd let you know, Merak,' he said. 'You can forget either Janine Jensen or Barbara Winton. I've been out to the *Trocadero*. Both women were definitely there the whole of last Friday night, playing roulette.'

'No chance of any of the witnesses being mistaken?'

'None whatsoever.'

'Then I guess we'll have to look to the mobs if we're to find the killer,' I said. 'And that isn't going to make things any easier.'

'You're right, it's not.' His tone was like an iron bar. 'Which is why I'm telling you to keep your nose out of this case. I've got enough on my plate without having to worry about what you're doing.'

He put the phone down. I sat staring at the receiver for several seconds before doing the same.

I told Dawn what he'd said. She looked disappointed, then shrugged.

'Well, as the old Chinese sage said, ' 'It's foolish to try to fight the inevitable'.'

'Sure,' I said. And that was when it hit me, right out of the blue.

'I've been a goddamned fool,' I told her. 'I should have picked it up before.'

'What are you talking about?'

'Maybe it's nothing at all, or maybe it's the lead I've been waiting for.' I got to my feet and jammed my hat back onto my head. 'First, I need to talk with someone.'

'Who?'

'Someone who might just lead me straight to the killer of Arlene, Ricardo and Jensen.'

'Hold on a minute, Johnny. I'm coming with you this time. Just to see you don't get yourself into any more trouble.'

I didn't like the idea one little bit but I knew that once she'd made up her mind about anything, there wasn't much I could do about it.

'Just a couple of details to attend to first,' I said. 'And then we'll go.'

Ten minutes later we were in the car and heading towards Bay City.

The big iron gates were still closed. I pushed them open and Dawn followed me inside.

'Whose place is this?' she asked.

'Arnold Henders.'

'You mean the lawyer who represented Charles Jensen at the divorce hearing?'

'The same.' I shifted my glance towards the palm trees. The table was there but there was no sign of Arnold. I guessed it was probably a little too early in the day for his siesta.

I walked up to the door and rapped on the glass panel. Footsteps sounded and the door opened. Mrs. Henders stood there and the expression on her face told me she wasn't too pleased to see me again.

'I thought I told you the last time not to come here again bothering my son with your questions,' she snapped.

'I'm sorry, but I'm afraid this is

important,' I said. 'A lot has happened since I last spoke to him. Charles Jensen has been murdered for one thing.'

'And what has that got to do with Arnold?' she demanded. Her face hadn't changed and she was still blocking the doorway.

'It could be nothing. It could be quite a lot. But until I've spoken to him, I won't know.'

For a moment, I thought she meant to slam the door in my face but then she thought better of it and stepped grudgingly to one side.

'Who's this?' she asked as Dawn followed me in. 'A woman cop?'

'My secretary,' I said. 'She does her best to keep me out of trouble.'

We went inside and she led us into the large living room. Arnold was seated near the window in his wheelchair.

'Ask your questions and then get out.' She spoke over her shoulder as she turned quickly for a woman of her build, and went out of the room.

Arnold eased his chair forward a couple of inches. There was an odd expression on his face. 'What is it you want to know?' he asked.

'I'd like you to tell me about three murders. But first, I want to go over what happened to you four years ago.'

'I've already told you that.'

I walked over to the fireplace. There was a heap of grey ashes in the wide grate. Across the top was a wide mantlepiece, the wood covered in a thick film of dust. Evidently Mrs. Hensen didn't believe in wasting time or energy in cleaning the place.

'I'm just here for a quiet little talk,' I said. 'Just to clear up a few loose ends that have been bothering me for some time now.'

I took out my .38 and placed it carefully on top of the mantel. 'You told me it could have been Arlene who tried to run you down, that she might have done it to get back at you for digging up all that false evidence of adultery.'

'That's correct.'

'Well you see, I don't think it was Arlene. I figure she was locked away someplace by that time. My guess is it was Charles Jensen in that car, wearing a black wig to look like Arlene.'

A curious expression moved across Arnold's face like the shadow of a cloud passing across the sun. 'Why would Jensen want to kill me? There was no reason for it.'

I moved slowly away from the fireplace. 'Oh, there was a very good reason. You were blackmailing him, threatening to tell about the dirt and lies you told in the divorce court about Arlene.'

'That's absolute nonsense.' His lips clamped down so tight they looked like the jaws of a vise. 'You're just clutching at straws now, Merak.'

'Am I? Then let me tell you something else I think. You got to know Arlene Jensen pretty well while you were working for her husband. In fact, I'd say you became infatuated with her. Maybe even more than that, you were obsessed by her. But she refused to have anything to do with you — and that really rankled.'

His hands were now clutching the sides of the wheelchair like clamps.

'So you brought her here, locked her

215

up in one of the upstairs rooms. If you couldn't have her by fair means, you meant to have her by foul.'

'This is all nothing more than supposition and conjecture on your part, Merak. You forget, I'm a lawyer. I know what constitutes real evidence and you've got none at all. In fact, I'd be quite within my rights phoning for the police and having you charged with slander and harassment.'

I walked past him to the window. His eyes never left me for a second.

'You know,' I said, 'it's a real pity your mother isn't much of a cleaner around the place.' I traced my finger along the layer of dust on the window sill. 'If she was, she'd have cleaned that Packard out there and you might have got away with these murders.'

'What has that car got to do with this yarn you're spinning?'

'Quite a lot. I noticed it the last time I was here but it didn't click them. In fact, I'd forgotten all about it until Dawn here happened to say something which brought it all back.'

'Me?' Dawn looked surprised. She had moved towards the far door through which Mrs. Henders had disappeared. 'What did I say?'

'You mentioned the old Chinese Sage who said one should never fight against the inevitable.'

'So?'

'Sage. The wheel rims and the bottom of that car are covered with mud and bits of sage. And the only place where that grows wild around here is up there in the hills where I was sapped and Arlene's body was dumped.'

I turned back to the window and pointed. 'I'd say you held the gun to Ricardo's back when he arranged to meet me there. Then your mother sat in the back of his car while you drove that Packard there with Arlene's body stashed in the boot.'

I heard Dawn's sharp exclamation a couple of seconds later and turned. Henders had leapt from his wheelchair and had crossed the room to the fireplace in half a dozen strides.

There was an ugly look on his face as

he snatched up the .38 I'd left there.

'You think you're smart, Merak. But this is as far as you go, both of you. I reckon I should have killed you instead of just coshing you.'

'But you had to take my gun and leave me alive so the cops would pin her murder on me,' I said.

'Unfortunately — yes. But I won't make the same mistake a second time.' He pointed the gun straight at me.

'You already have,' I said. 'That gun is empty. It was just a ploy to put an end to this paralysis charade of yours.' I slid my right hand into my jacket pocket and took out the old revolver I sometimes used as a spare. 'But this one isn't.'

He aimed the .38 at my head and squeezed the trigger. There was a faint click but that was all. For a moment, I thought he was going to throw the gun at me but a sudden commotion at the door stopped him.

Mrs. Henders came charging through the door like a maddened bull. She held a shotgun in both hands. It looked as though it could stop a rampaging elephant. I reckon she'd have blown my head off with it but at the last moment, Dawn stuck out a shapely leg and gave her a push in the middle of the back.

The woman uttered a shriek like a demented banshee and sailed across the room, flailing with her arms. The gun flew out of her hands and landed near my feet while she smashed into the table with a crash that could have been heard the other side of L.A. She twitched for a moment and then lay still.

'You'd better put that gun down and get her onto the couch,' I said to Henders. 'Then you sit down right beside her.'

I guess he knew when he was on to a bad roll of the dice for he did exactly as he was told. Breathing hard, he pulled her onto the couch and flopped down at her side. She lay with her head back, eyes closed.

I pulled up one of the chairs, spun it round, and sat down. 'I figure I've got the full picture now,' I said. 'Correct me if I'm wrong about any of the details. You dug up the dirt on Arlene and any you couldn't find, you invented. Then after the divorce, you decided to do two things — blackmail Jensen by threatening to spill everything to the D.A. and kidnap Arlene for yourself. It must have been hell for her, pocked up here all these years, kept a prisoner for your own sadistic pleasure.'

'It wasn't like that at all.' He ran his tongue around his lips. 'I loved her, much more than her husband did.'

For a moment, I almost believed him. Maybe, in his own twisted fashion, he had loved Arlene but that would soon turn to hate once she rejected him.

'Then things went wrong,' I continued. 'She made a break for it. That was when you finally realized that keeping her here could be dangerous. You had to kill her. But you had to get rid of the body. Somehow, you found out that Ricardo was feeding me with information about Jensen so you hatched your plan to get me up there and finger me for her murder.

'It needed two cars, of course. Yours and Ricardo's. By this time, Arlene was tucked away in the boot of the Packard, which you drove. Your mother told me she couldn't drive and I believe her. She went with Ricardo in his, holding a gun on him. Ricardo was probably in on the scheme at the beginning, maybe you'd promised him a heap of dough to help you. But that wasn't in your itinerary. After you slugged him, you rigged it to look like suicide. Then Arlene was dumped next to me and my gun taken and one shot fired. Since Arlene was killed here there was no chance of the cops finding the murder slug.'

'And why would I want to kill Jensen?' His voice was as cold as midnight in the Arctic now.

I shrugged. 'I can think of a number of reasons. You'd already figured out it was him who ran you down. He'd probably stopped paying the blackmail. That would make him very dangerous where you were concerned.'

Mrs. Henders stirred. Her slack mouth opened and closed like a fish. Then her eyes opened. They were like polished agate. With an effort, she heaved herself into a sitting position, glaring at me.

'I've just been explaining to your son how you both murdered three people,' I said. 'But I guess you know it all. Now you're back with us, I think we'll just sit here, nice and quiet, until the cops arrive.'

Still keeping the revolver on them, I got up and went to the phone. I dialled Lieutenant O'Leary's number.

THE END

We do hope that you have enjoyed reading this large print book.

Did you know that all of our titles are available for purchase?

We publish a wide range of high quality large print books including:
Romances, Mysteries, Classics
General Fiction
Non Fiction and Westerns

Special interest titles available in large print are:
The Little Oxford Dictionary
Music Book, Song Book
Hymn Book, Service Book

Also available from us courtesy of Oxford University Press:
Young Readers' Dictionary
(large print edition)
Young Readers' Thesaurus
(large print edition)

For further information or a free brochure, please contact us at:
Ulverscroft Large Print Books Ltd.,
The Green, Bradgate Road, Anstey,
Leicester, LE7 7FU, England.
Tel: (00 44) **0116 236 4325**
Fax: (00 44) **0116 234 0205**

A TIME FOR MURDER

John Glasby

Carlos Galecci, a top man in organized crime, has been murdered — and the manner of his death is extraordinary . . . He'd last been seen the previous night, entering his private vault, to which only he knew the combination. When he fails to emerge by the next morning, his staff have the metal door cut open — to discover Galecci dead with a knife in his back. Private detective Johnny Merak is hired to find the murderer and discover how the impossible crime was committed — but is soon under threat of death himself . . .

THE MASTER MUST DIE

John Russell Fearn

Gyron de London, a powerful industrialist of the year 2190, receives a letter warning him of his doom on the 30th March, three weeks hence. Despite his precautions — being sealed in a guarded, radiation-proof cube — he dies on the specified day, as forecast! When scientific investigator Adam Quirke is called to investigate, he discovers that de London had been the victim of a highly scientific murder — but who was the murderer, and how was this apparently impossible crime committed?

MONTENEGRIN GOLD

Brian Ball

Discovering his late father's war diaries, Charles Copley learns that he had been involved in counter-intelligence. When Charles is approached by an organisation trying to buy the diaries, he refuses. But he is viciously attacked — and then his son is murdered . . . Seeking revenge, he is joined by Maria Wright, daughter of his father's wartime friend. They are led on a journey to the mountains of Montenegro — and thirty years back in time in search of a lost treasure.